Fractured Images

Barbara McLain

Archway Publishing books may be ordered through booksellers or by contacting:

Archway Publishing
1663 Liberty Drive
Bloomington, IN 47403
www.archwaypublishing.com
844-669-3957

ISBN: 978-1-6657-0420-5 (sc)
ISBN: 978-1-6657-0421-2 (e)

Library of Congress Control Number: 2021905124

Print information available on the last page.

Archway Publishing rev. date: 03/22/2021

To my daughter Kara. You were a gift in the past and a light for the future. You will always be the cherry on top.

Everyone occasionally is haunted by the past and should consider; no amount of remorse will erase the past and no amount of apprehension will alter the future.

—R J Intindola (Gandolfo), 1979

Deidra Wentworth

She popped in her contacts; green eyes staring back at her amidst a frothy mass of cleansing foam. She rinsed, splashed, and applied moisturizer. Her reflection looked back through the ornate bathroom mirror. Next came the toner, the eye cream, and foundation. A bronze clock ticked away the seconds in the corner of the granite countertop. Carefully, the eyebrow pencil was applied, followed by concealer under her eyes, and liner on her lids. Mascara came next. Finally, she brushed on setting powder, added a bit of highlighter, and applied a deep rose-pink lipstick. She removed the towel from her wet hair and rubbed in an ample amount of gel. The noise of the blow-dryer drowned out the ticking clock, until her long blonde hair shone like gold. She quickly checked her roots in the mirror and decided they looked fine. A few loose waves of curl, and Deidra Wentworth was ready to be seen by others.

Just as she reached to flip off the long chrome and

crystal bath light, she noticed a tiny crack crawling up the mirror from behind the clock. *Where did that come from?* Irritated that a minuscule crack would invade her pristine space, she resolved to replace the elaborate mirror.

Deidra's slender body left the bathroom and went through her dressing room, out the lavish bedroom, and down the wide, circular staircase. On the shiny kitchen bar of the extravagant house in Quinley Park, Texas, a wealthy suburb of Dallas, a newspaper lay open to the society page. "Sterling Wentworth Estate Settled," she read the headline. "Good Lord," she murmured, picking up the paper.

> The estate of the late Sterling and Patricia Wentworth was settled last week with the entire sum rewarded to their only daughter, Deidra Wentworth of Quinley Park, Texas. The vice president of Dehlco Petroleum Corporation and his wife were killed when their private plane went down five months ago.

Deidra rolled her eyes with disgust and folded up the paper. A warm cinnamon roll and cup of coffee awaited her at the bar. She heard the doorbell chime and the footsteps of the housekeeper, Susan Toll, scurry to see who was there.

"Deidra!" The voice of Vance Montgomery reverberated through the foyer and into the kitchen. In swaggered the young man, his auburn hair combed straight back from his forehead, not a strand out of place. He held a copy of the newspaper. "Did you see the *Daily Reporter*?" he asked and waved the paper in front of her. "You made the society page."

Deidra shoved it aside. "I saw it," she said with distaste. "I wish they hadn't made a headline out of it. It's bad enough having lost both my parents suddenly without a reminder from the printed page."

Vance took his place at the bar next to her and gave her a quick kiss on the cheek. Without being asked, Susan poured him a cup of coffee.

"So how is it staying in the house again?" Vance asked.

"A bit spooky, really."

"So are Sterling and Pat haunting the place?" he teased.

"Not in that way, although I miss Daddy terribly," she replied, licking off her fingers. "It's just all the memories from my youth. This place makes me feel like a teenager again." Taking a quick glance around, she whispered, "And Susan doesn't help matters."

"Did she scold you for something?"

"It's the looks she gives me. I feel guilty leaving fingerprints on the refrigerator."

"Get over it," he advised. He took a bite of her cinnamon roll. "It's your place now. Do what you want to with it. Have some fun, my dear."

He smiled and gave her a wink.

"It's time for me to get to the office," he announced. He was employed by Montgomery Financial Group, which his father, Lawrence Montgomery owned. "You won't be lonely, will you?"

"India's coming by this afternoon. Maybe we can go through some of the stuff in this house."

"When will you be going back to work?"

Deidra shrugged. "Soon. I need to get out."

She worked for Alistair-Borne Publishing House in Dallas. Her father had arranged her employment after she graduated from Southern Methodist University six years ago.

India Morelli and Deidra had been friends since childhood. When she arrived that afternoon, Susan served them fruit cups and coffee at the mahogany dining table.

"I saw the newspaper article," India said, pushing her black hair behind her ear. "Just what you wanted, I'm sure."

"All I want is to get on with life. Mother and Daddy's death has been a long, drawn-out ordeal."

"I can tell you this: When Britt and I broke up six months ago, I thought it was the most devastating thing ever. But when your parents went down in that plane, it put things in a totally different perspective. If there is ever anything you need, I promise I'll do what I can," India added.

Deidra returned an appreciative smile.

Although India had been in the house many times, Deidra led her from room to room. They stood in the sunlight that beamed through the floor-to-ceiling windows of the music room. A grand piano stood majestically upon an extravagant oriental rug.

"I spent a good part of my youth right here," Deidra said.

"I remember you practicing for hours."

"Not by choice," Deidra reminded her friend.

"Play something," India suggested. "I miss hearing you."

Deidra sat down and played a few measures of Mozart's "Piano Sonata."

"Don't stop," India begged. "I still think you should have majored in music instead of journalism."

Deidra shrugged.

"You only went into journalism because your mother wanted you to study music."

"Well, maybe," Deidra confessed. "Mother and I never saw eye to eye."

"I remember."

India followed Deidra up the curving stairway to the bedroom that had belonged to her parents.

"It still smells like them," Deidra said. She drew open the drapes to let in some natural light. "I don't think I'll be sleeping in here. I can't imagine making love in my parents' room. The idea gives me chills."

India laughed. "So what will you use it for? You need to make this house your own, Deidra. What do you want to turn it into?"

"Maybe I could turn this room into an office. I could sit in here and read manuscripts for work. The lighting is great. I could light the fireplace in the evening and read quietly."

"That sounds wonderful. Change the drapes, paint the walls, get new decor ..."

"Brynn," Deidra interrupted. "I can get Brynn to help decorate. That's what she does for a living, and she's the best in the business."

"Brynn would love it," agreed India.

Two days later, India returned, accompanied by Brynn Montgomery. Brynn carried in a satchel filled with fabric swatches and paint samples. She was Vance Montgomery's sister. Brynn, India, and Deidra had all attended high school together and then followed Vance to SMU for college. They remained best of friends.

Brynn opened the satchel and arranged her samples on the dining room table. "I am totally excited about this," she squealed. Her dark-red hair was cut short and spiky. Earrings dangled next to her face. "I love decorating. Doing it for a friend is even more exciting. Oh, Deidra, we can turn this place into a reflection of you. Now, I've got traditional samples, modern samples, and some unique samples. Do you feel more comfortable with warm colors or cool colors?"

They hauled samples throughout the house while reminiscing about past adventures. "Remember how we skipped in high school and went downtown?" Brynn asked.

"And don't forget when I talked you into running off to Europe after graduation," Deidra reminded her.

"My mother still hasn't forgiven you for that," Brynn said. "She still thinks you're a bad influence on me."

"What about Deidra's influence on your brother?" India asked.

Brynn shrugged. "She's not real hep on that, either, but I guess Vance can take care of himself."

The afternoon passed quickly. Susan prepared a light supper, which the women enjoyed around the pool.

"Brynn, I can't tell you how excited I am now about fixing up the house," said Deidra.

"You need something to be excited about." Brynn gave her friend a hug.

Just then, the telephone rang. Susan's voice came through the intercom that the call was for Deidra. She dashed inside to take the call.

"Vance, is that you?"

There was a brief silence on the other end and then she heard a deep, slow voice say, "You don't know me, but I know you. I knew your father. And he owed me a lot of money. Now, it's your turn to settle our differences. Cooperate and you won't get hurt." Click.

"Hello? Hello? Who the hell are you?" There was dead silence on the other end.

Unidentified Female

Sirens sounded. Ambulance lights strobed across the entrance to the emergency room at St. Rafael Hospital in Wichita, Kansas. In a flurry of activity, the crew rushed a gurney inside.

"Female, approximately twenty-eight, found unresponsive at the scene," the voice of a paramedic called out.

Without delay, hospital personnel rushed to their positions.

"Intubated at the scene. Neurologically a GCS 3T. Pulse 50, BP 100/60. There appears to be an indentation in the left temporal area of the skull, fractured left humerus, deep lacerations to left side of the face, arm, and upper leg."

"Maintain dopamine drip. Place on monitor and respirator," ordered the trauma doctor.

Bright lights and beeping sounds reflected the urgency of the moment.

"We'll need a head CT, stat. CBC, chemistries. Type and cross 6 units FFP and blood products, fourteen packed platelets on call to OR."

Beep ... beep ... beep. She gradually became aware of low-speaking voices, although their messages were meaningless. At first, she could not determine her own position. Was she sitting, lying down, or completely upside-down? It was as if she had no body.

"Hello, there." The voice sounded distant, yet it was soft and soothing.

She tried to open her eyes, but they would not cooperate. A soft humming accompanied the sensation of a light touch somewhere indistinguishable on her motionless body.

There was sound. There was movement and touch. The warmth of a gentle hand stroked her face. Gradually, she focused on a round, brown face with a wide smile that stretched toward two beautiful amber eyes, which were looking upon her.

"Hello, dear," the nurse said. "I've been waiting to see those pretty grey eyes of yours for a long time. You don't know me, but I've been caring for you about three weeks now. My name is Adelle Hall. I'm anxious to find out who you are."

Once again, sleep drew her away.

The next time her eyes opened, she was greeted by a group of five people gathered around her bed. They were all smiling, even laughing, and celebrating her revival. Every one of them was dressed in various colors and designs of scrubs, and each wore a name tag.

A partially bald, gray-haired man wearing a lab coat and glasses leaned over and spoke to her.

"I'm Dr. Dean Milton," he said, grinning. "You're quite famous around here. It's been a long journey, and you have a long road ahead of you, but we are here. We are all here to help you."

She tried to speak, but nothing came out.

"You were in an accident and brought here to St. Rafael Hospital. You are in Wichita, Kansas," Dr. Milton filled her in.

"You've been in a coma for three weeks," Adelle added.

"Are you able to tell us who you are?" the doctor asked.

She studied the strangers at the foot of her bed before they disbursed to their stations in the Neurological Intensive Care Unit. Only Adelle and Dr. Milton remained, checking vitals and filling out charts. She became aware of tubes and needles protruding from her body. Monitors of various sizes cluttered the small curtained-off space. Her left arm, she realized, was in a cast. With her right hand, she felt her face and discovered that her head was wrapped in a tight dressing. On the whiteboard next to her bed were listed times and numbers, but on the top, instead of a name, it read 156UFKS.

"Is there anything you need?" asked Adelle.

A small voice whispered, "'ank ooh."

Breaking into her wide smile, Adelle responded, "You are very welcome."

The next day she was more alert, aware of her hurting body. Dr. Milton stood at her bedside.

"You were in a car accident twenty-two days ago and were admitted in critical condition. You have two broken ribs and a broken arm. Your face, left arm, and upper leg were badly cut, but they have been stitched and should heal nicely. Do you understand?"

She nodded.

The doctor gently placed his hand over hers and looked into her eyes. "You also have a traumatic brain injury. We had to do surgery. Time will tell how extensive the damage is. Do you have any memory of the accident?"

She shook her head the best she could.

"Can you tell me your name?"

Her voice was weak. "I don't know."

"Can you give me the name of a family member or friend we can call?"

Her expression was blank, as if the question did not register.

Dr. Milton smiled. "Your body has been through a lot. Rest is your best friend right now."

As he moved from the bedside, a weak but clear voice said, "I'm hungry."

The doctor laughed out loud. "We will get you something to eat."

Adelle removed the tube, and her patient began to eat; as she attended to her, she hummed a vaguely familiar tune.

"What is that song?" she asked.

"The song I'm humming? That, my dear, is 'Amazing Grace.' It's an old hymn I've known since childhood. You like it?"

"It's nice," she replied. "Can you tell me what 156UFKS means?"

Adelle looked confused until the patient pointed to the whiteboard on the wall.

"That's who you are."

Once again, the patient looked confused.

"When they brought you in," explained the nurse, "we didn't know your name. So 156UFKS is your identification number. It means Unidentified Female in Kansas."

"I don't remember my name," she said, "but I don't think it's that."

Adelle let out a hearty laugh. "I suppose not. Until you remember, what would you rather be called?"

~

At last, she was moved to a regular room.

"We'll miss you in ICU," Adelle told her. "But we're still on the same floor, so I'll be in to see you."

"I hope so. You're the only person I know."

Adelle sat in a chair next to her. "You won't be alone," she promised. "Did you decide what you would like to be called?"

The patient pondered the question, smiled, and replied, "I want to be called Amazing Grace."

Adelle threw her head back in laughter. "That's a wonderful name. I'll tell everyone to call you Grace. And you are indeed amazing."

~

One morning, shortly after a sponge bath, a tall woman carrying a clipboard entered her room. She wore a pink pantsuit and a nametag that read "Laura Huffman, LCSW." She greeted the patient with a firm handshake.

"I'm the hospital social worker," she said. "Will it be okay if I ask you a few questions?"

"I guess so."

Laura Huffman pulled a chair to the bedside.

"Have you been able to remember your name?"

The patient shook her head, tired of hearing that question.

"I see. Do you know where you live?"

"Right now, I live here," she said.

"I mean before your car accident."

"I don't remember anything. I don't know if I have a family or friends. Do I have children? Am I married? I don't know if I belong anywhere or even if anyone is sad that I am here."

"That's what I will help you figure out, honey."

"My name's not Honey. At least I don't think it is. Would you call me Grace?"

"Is Grace your name?"

"I have no idea, but I doubt that my name is Honey or that long UF number they gave me."

"I bet you're right." Ms. Hoffman looked at her as if she were a child. "I will call you Grace. At least until we find out who you really are."

Just as the social worker stood to leave, Dr. Milton arrived. "Hello, Laura," he said. He nodded a smile to the patient.

"Her name is Grace," Hoffman told him.

"Grace?" he said. "So, you figured out your name?"

"Grace is the name she wants to be called."

"Then Grace we shall call you," he agreed. The doctor

stood behind the social worker so Grace could easily see them both. He proceeded to ask her a series of questions.

"Can you tell me what time the clock shows?"

"Ten fifty-three," Grace replied correctly.

"That's great," Laura cried. "You passed that one."

Dr. Milton glanced at the social worker. "These are not pass or fail questions. We just want to establish the condition of Grace's brain."

"Can you tell me who the president is?"

Grace shook her bandaged head.

"Do you remember your parents' names?"

There was no memory of parents.

Dr. Milton handed her a book. "Read me a page," he instructed.

Grace opened the book to a random page and began to read.

> "When you are a Bear of Very Little Brain, and you Think of Things, you find sometimes that a Thing which seems very Thingish inside you is quite different when it gets out into the open and has other people looking at it."
>
> "And if anyone knows anything about anything," said Bear to himself, "it's Owl who knows something about something," he said, "or my name's not Winnie-the-Pooh," he said. "Which it is," he added. "So, there you are." (A. A. Milne, *Winnie-the-Pooh*).

Grace laughed. "What is this book?" She looked at the cover and read, "*Winnie-the-Pooh* by A. A. Milne. Who drew these charming illustrations? E. H. Shepard," she read. "I like that name. Maybe my last name is Shepard. That's a nice name."

"We have hope," Ms. Hoffman said, "that eventually we will discover who you really are."

Several times a day, a nurse helped Grace out of bed so she could practice walking. Difficult at first, it grew easier with practice. She began to spend more time sitting up in a chair than in her bed. Each day, she worked with an occupational therapist who had her practice body movement, holding a pencil, and using stairs.

One day, after Dr. Milton removed the wrapping from her head, Grace discovered that she had no hair.

"I'm bald!" she exclaimed.

The doctor smiled. "Your hair was shaved for surgery. It will grow back."

A small bandage replaced the head wrap. He uncovered the lacerations on her face, arm, and upper leg, which were healing well.

"What do I look like?" she asked.

Sitting up straight, she craned her neck to view herself in the mirror. At first glance, she presumed that the mirror was cracked. Seconds later, she realized that the crack was in her own face. A scar ran from mid-temple to her jaw line. Her bald head sported a web of stitches.

Dr. Milton pulled a chair up, so Grace was at eye level.

"You are one tough person," he told her. "When they brought you in, your chances of survival were exceedingly small. But look at you." His hand on her chin, he gently turned her head from side to side. "Your condition is what we call complete declarative amnesia, or CDA. It is quite rare, the result of severe trauma to the temporal lobe of the brain. Your procedural memory is intact. That's why you remember the name of objects, how to read, and how to tie your shoes. However, your declarative memory, which has to do with recall and experiences, appears to be gone. You have no recall of past experiences or relationships."

"Will it come back?" Grace asked.

"It may never return. I'm going to contact Dr. Ted Yates. He's a psychiatrist and can help you deal with all of this."

"How will I know if I have a family? Do I have kids? A husband? Do I work somewhere?"

"Slow down," said Dr. Milton. "When you came in, you were not wearing a ring, so we assume you are not married. After a physical exam, it was determined that you have never given birth; you also have no wisdom teeth or tonsils. You did, however, have chicken pox, as indicated by several scars on your arms and back."

"Knock, knock." In walked Laura Hoffman. She handed a paper to the doctor.

His eyebrows lifted as he said, "Oh, really?"

They looked at Grace, and Laura smiled; she said, "We may have a lead on who you are."

Deidra Wentworth

"Don't worry about it," Vance said when Deidra told him about the phone call. "Probably someone playing a prank on you."

"It wasn't a very funny prank," she responded as she held two of Brynn's swatches up to the window in her new bedroom. "What if they know I'm alone here?"

"Susan's here."

"Only in the daytime." She decided the sage green swatch looked better than the rose-beige.

"You have an alarm system, Dee," Vance reminded her. "Blow it off. Relax."

"Which do you prefer, the sage or the beige?" She chuckled. "That sounds like a poem."

"That's better. Laugh a little." He stood behind her and wrapped his arms around her waist. "You have nothing to worry about."

"So what color do you like?" she asked again.

Vance walked over to the bed and plopped down onto it. "I like …; I like the idea of me being here with you."

"Well, you're here now," she said.

He reached for her arm, leading her to the bed beside him. "I mean all the time."

She smiled as he drew nearer. "I need you, Dee." He kissed her softly on the lips. "I need you really bad."

The next kiss was deeper. He caressed her blonde hair as she made circles with her finger on his back. Just then, his cell phone rang. Breaking their embrace, he checked the number.

"One moment." He answered the phone.

Returning to work was a relief for Deidra. The office provided a familiar refuge, with no ghosts of her deceased parents. The smell of manuscripts waiting for her to review felt like a greeting from old friends.

"Welcome back." Arthur Wexler leaned into her open door. Arthur, another editor at Alastair-Borne Publishing House, flashed his thin grin. His slender body was outfitted in his signature pleated khakis and a long-sleeved button-down striped shirt. "So sorry about your parents," he said. "You were certainly missed around here. If there's anything I can do to help you get back on board, just say the word.

"Thank you, Arthur. That's kind of you."

"I mean it."

Deidra knew he did mean it. Arthur was a kind and gentle soul.

"Were you able to sell your condo and move to your

parents' house in Quinley Park?" He ran his thin fingers through his flat brown hair.

"I did sell the condo. One less thing to worry about," she stated.

He stared at her for a moment before saying, "I'm so glad you're back."

Deidra's phone sounded, and she answered in her perkiest voice.

Arthur could tell that it was no one she was expecting to hear from. Deidra's expression slid from disappointment to fear. She ended the call without saying a word.

"Are you okay?" Arthur asked.

Deidra was visibly shaking. Arthur reached for her hand, squeezing it with concern.

"Just give me a moment," she said. "I'll be fine."

"Who was that?"

"A prank call," she told him. "Just a prank call."

Deidra found it hard to focus on work the rest of the day. Every time her phone rang, a pang of fear sliced through her. She decided to call India.

"How about meeting at Bowie's after work?" Deidra suggested. "We can celebrate my first day back." She listened to the reply. "Great. I'll see you there."

Deidra felt a sense of reprieve when she joined her friend at a corner table in their favorite bar and grill. Bowie's was the place they went to unwind.

"I'm in need of nachos and a strawberry daiquiri," she told India.

"That sounds perfect," India agreed. "So how was your first day back?"

"It was fine. A pile of work was waiting for me."

"And Arthur, how was Arthur?"

"Arthur was Arthur. He's a really nice person," Deidra said.

"Just nerdy," India added.

"Very nerdy," Deidra agreed.

They munched on the cheesy chips and sipped their drinks.

"You're quieter than I expected you to be," India observed. "What is it?"

Deidra shrugged. "It's nothing."

"Tell me," she demanded.

"I'm sure it's nothing, but I got a phone call today. It was a man's voice. He told me that I own my father's debt to him and that I'd better cooperate."

India's mouth dropped in astonishment. "What debt?"

"I have no idea what he's talking about. I have copies of Daddy's financial records from his accounts."

"What else did he say?"

"Nothing. I hung up."

"Deidra, that's a threat," said India.

"Is it?"

"You should call the police."

"I don't want to make a big deal out of it. Vance told me to blow it off."

"Oh, Vance. What does he know? Did it scare you?"

"Well, yes," Deidra confessed. "I haven't thought of anything else since."

India took out her cell.

"What are you doing?" Deidra asked.

"I'm doing nothing, but you are calling the police." India punched in a few numbers and handed the phone to her friend.

Deidra gave her name and then described the calls she

had received, one on her home phone and one to her cell. Quietly she waited through the reply. "But I don't know who it is," she said. "I see. Well, thanks anyway." She handed the phone back to India.

"What did they say?" India asked.

In an irritated voice, Deidra replied, "They said that there is nothing they can do until a crime has been committed."

"That'll be too late," India exclaimed.

"If I knew who it was, I could put a restraining order on them. It could be anyone," Deidra said.

Both women glanced around the bar and grill, wondering if someone in Bowies could be the culprit.

The Blue Royale offered a quiet atmosphere compared to Bowie's. Deidra and Vance talked softly as candlelight danced across their faces.

"Has anything changed at work while you were gone?" Vance asked.

"Not much, and I'm glad of that." She paused, glancing around the dim room.

"Deidra? Are you okay?"

"I'm fine," she replied, trying to shake off her preoccupation with the strange phone calls.

After several minutes of silence, Vance asked, with an annoyed tone, "What is wrong?"

"I got another call," she told him.

"A call from whom?"

"Another threatening call, Vance. Just like the other

day, only on my cell this time. It was a man's voice. He told me I owe him my father's debt, and I better cooperate."

"Did he give you a name?"

"No name. It really scares me."

The waiter placed their meals before them. Taking her first bite of salad, Deidra got a whiff of the seafood platter in front of Vance.

"You got seafood?" she asked, turning up her nose.

"What's wrong with that?" Vance asked.

"You ought to know by now that seafood, even the smell of it, makes me nauseous."

"You never told me that,"

She snapped, "I've told you many times. I choked on a fish bone when I was twelve and cannot tolerate it since. It's so insensitive of you, Vance."

"Sorry," he grumbled.

After a few solemn bites, he said, "I hope you know how important you are to me. I mean, you're the only thing I think about."

Deidra gave him a slight smile.

"Look around, Dee. No one else in this whole place can hold a candle to you. I know those calls have scared you, and I don't want to see you frightened." He took her hand and looked into her eyes. "That's why I believe the time is right for me to move in with you. I will protect you, babe."

He leaned across the small table and kissed her. She backed away quickly.

"That fish," she exclaimed. "I can't stand fish-breath."

He laughed. "Okay, I'll brush my teeth when we get back to your place then, I am going to ravage you."

"Your mother won't be thrilled," she said.

"My mother? She doesn't need to know."

Deidra laughed. "I mean, she won't like you moving in with me."

"Don't let Mother bother you, she ..." His sentence was interrupted by his phone. He looked at the number and said, "I better take this one."

He answered the phone in his serious, businesslike voice and walked to the corner of the restaurant to talk. Deidra sighed and helped herself to a dinner roll.

Grace

"We have received a missing person's report," explained Laura Hoffman. "A female, age thirty-one, went missing six weeks ago. She lives two counties over."

Grace gave her a blank stare. Was she supposed to be excited or worried?

"Is that who I am?" she asked.

Dr. Milton spoke up. "It's a missing person's report. No more, no less. Try not to worry about it. I'm going to contact Dr. Yates. He can help you sort out all you've been going through." As he moved toward the doorway to leave, he said, "In time we will figure out who you are."

Grace turned to the social worker. "Is there a description of the missing woman?"

"Her blood type is O positive, just like yours. And she has a scar on the inside of her left forearm." Laura glanced down at Grace's left arm, which was wrapped in a cast.

"When will you know if it's me?"

"We'll contact law enforcement and go from there. Hopefully, we'll know before you leave us."

"Leave?" Grace was astonished. "When am I leaving? Where will I go?"

"Relax," Laura said calmly. "I don't know how much longer you will be here. When you are ready, you will be sent to a rehabilitation center. But not until you're ready."

After Laura left her room, Grace began to realize how much she missed Adelle in ICU. Adelle made Grace feel important, like a friend. Laura made her feel like a case attached to her clipboard.

Grace grew stronger every day. She walked the blue and gray hospital hallway, memorizing every picture on the wall. She began to recognize family members of other patients. Some were loud and argumentative. Others appeared close and supportive. She wished that they were her family. Many of the rooms were filled with flowers and balloons. It occurred to her that she had not received a single card.

One morning as she sat in her room, there was a knock on the door. Looking up, she saw a huge arrangement of flowers.

"Surprise!" Adelle peeked out from behind the bouquet; her wide smile shone like the sun.

"Adelle! I've missed you. Who are the flowers for?"

"They're for you, dear." She set the arrangement on the windowsill.

"Beautiful!" Grace proclaimed. "Just beautiful. Other

rooms have flowers, but I didn't think I would get any. After all, I have no family that I know of."

Adelle squeezed Grace's hand. "I'm your family. Me and Dr. Milton and many others around here."

Grace smiled, and Adelle sat across from her on the edge of the bed.

"Tell me what's happening," the nurse said.

"What can happen in a hospital? I walk the halls, I read a little. Mrs. Hoffman's been in to see me."

"Mrs. Hoffman?"

"Yes," said Grace. "Laura Hoffman, the hospital social worker. She told me that they received a missing person's report about a woman about my age with the same blood-type."

"Do they think that's who you are?" Adelle asked.

"They don't know. They must wait and see. I wish I knew more about her. I don't know how to feel about it."

"Don't feel anything," Adelle advised. "Just wait and see." She picked up a magazine and saw that Grace had finished a crossword puzzle. "That's great," she said. "You figured the whole thing out."

"I cheated," said Grace sheepishly. "I looked up the answers in the back. If I knew the answers once, I don't anymore. It's funny. I can read, but I don't remember learning how. I can work the remote control, but I don't recognize anything on TV."

"Then it's all new to you, dear. Enjoy exploring the world. Be curious. Be fascinated. Just like a small child."

"But I'm not a small child," Grace reminded her.

"In a way, your life began again that day I first saw your pretty gray eyes. Remember how everyone had been waiting to meet you? They gathered around your bed to greet you. Think about how Dr. Milton cared for you until your body was ready to live again. One step at a time, baby. One step at a time."

~

The consultation room was dimly lit by two table lamps. The walls were painted cool, soothing shades of blue and green. A painting on the wall depicted a quiet path through the woods. Grace sat on a couch, taking in the peaceful setting.

The door swung open, and in walked a tall, slender man with a smile that creased his entire face. Bald on top, the rest of his white hair hung down to his shoulders. When he turned to close the door behind him, Grace noticed a ponytail in the back of his head. He was dressed in jeans and a denim shirt that was unbuttoned partway down his chest, making it easy to see his hemp necklace with a turquoise stone. He introduced himself.

"Grace, I am Dr. Ted Yates. I'm so glad to meet you." He folded himself into the chair opposite her. "Call me Dr. Ted," he said. "Dr. Milton thought it a good idea for us to talk about things. Tell me what you've experienced."

Grace took a deep breath and launched into her story, beginning with the moment she opened her eyes and saw the ICU staff at the foot of her bed, to her surprise when Adelle brought her flowers.

"You have no recollection of your previous life? No recollection of the accident? Have you discovered any names or places that ring a bell in your mind?" All the answers were no. Dr. Ted continued, "Tell me how you're feeling about all of this."

"I don't know," said Grace. "I'm empty. Sometimes I feel confused. Sometimes scared. Often lonely."

"Those are all reasonable emotions for what you're going through," he responded. "Allow yourself to feel them. You know, when any of us loses someone close, we grieve. You have lost everyone you were close to, even though you don't remember them. You've also lost yourself."

There was a pause in the conversation. Grace didn't know what to say. Finally, Dr. Ted spoke again.

"I talked to Dr. Milton at length and did some research on complete declarative amnesia. There's not much information out there. From what I understand, your brain will never be as it was before. It is perfectly functional, but a big chunk is now missing. In a way, it's like starting all over. We'll see if we can tap into any memories, but it might be more beneficial to figure out, not who you were, but who you want to be now."

"Adelle said I was like a newborn."

"You mentioned her before."

"She's my friend from ICU. She says she's my family now."

The doctor smiled. "Good for Adelle. Is she someone you can talk to?"

"She is. She's kind," Grace said.

Dr. Ted pulled out a stack of picture cards with the name of the pictures on the back. He held up one picture at a time. Grace was able to name many of them such as car, dog, and house. She had some difficulty naming a ladder and a fly swatter. When he turned the cards over and held up each word, Grace could read them easily.

"You know this is a dog," he said. "Do you recall an experience you've had with a dog?"

"Dogs are soft," she replied. "They wag their tails."

"What might be a good name for a dog?" he asked.

Grace thought. "Maybe that dog could be called Brownie? It's brown."

"What would Brownie do?"

"Bark?" She was responding with questions.

"What kind of cars do you like?" he inquired, holding up another card.

"What?" She could not grasp his question.

"Well, do you like compact cars, luxury cars, ATVs?"

"I have no idea what that is."

The session ended after a while; Grace was exhausted. "Too much thinking," she told Dr. Ted.

"It's like exercise for your brain. The more you do it, the stronger it will get."

~

Dr. Milton listened carefully to Grace's heart. He took her pulse and examined what was left of her lacerations.

"You are the most amazing patient I have ever worked with," he told her. "Your recovery has been remarkable."

"I wish my hair would grow back." Tiny wisps of brown hair were beginning to sprout from her scalp. The cut on her face had healed into a thick, raised scar.

The doctor put away his stethoscope. He crossed his arms and smiled at Grace.

"There's not much more we can do for you here," he told her.

"Where will I go?" She could not remember being anywhere but St. Rafael Hospital.

"We'll be transferring you to Crestway Rehabilitation Center."

"Where's that?"

"It's here in Wichita. The good folks at Crestway will work with you to recover some skills you will need to know. They will teach you to cook, to keep house, and to manage money."

"I know about money," Grace said.

"Do you remember buying anything with it? Do you recall standing in a checkout line?"

Those memories were gone.

"Why do I remember some things but not other things?" she asked with a tone of aggravation.

Dr. Milton gave a deep sigh. "Your brain was seriously damaged. Basically, part of your brain is no longer functioning. That's the part that retained your experiences. You may remember many of the processes you learned: walking, writing, reading, and such. But memories of places you went, activities you took part in, and people you had relationships with are gone."

"Can they call me Grace at this Crestway place, or do I have to go by that number?"

"They will call you whatever we put on the transfer orders," Dr. Milton told her. "Think about a last name. Mrs. Hoffman will be in with the papers soon. But first, let's get that cast off your arm."

Rain pelted the window of Grace's hospital room. She looked out and could see cars splashing by, sending a spray of water over the curb. She wondered what it would feel like to be out in the rain. Her thoughts were interrupted when Laura Hoffman entered, clipboard and all.

They sat down opposite each other while Laura explained the transfer papers.

"You'll like it at Crestway," the social worker guaranteed. "They are nice people over there. You will continue your sessions with Dr. Yates as well. Now, what name would you like me to put on the form?"

"Put Grace."

"You like the name Grace?" Laura printed the name on the line.

"It reminds me of the song Adelle sings."

"That's nice. How about a last name?" Laura asked, suggesting, "Maybe Green, like the color of the walls. Or perhaps Smith, or Wells?"

"Shepard," Grace interrupted. "I like the name Shepard. I saw some illustrations by someone named Shepard. They were simple and sweet."

"And middle initial?"

"What?" Grace didn't understand.

"Most people have a middle name. Mine is Louise. The form asks for the first letter of your middle name."

"I have no idea," Grace said.

"We can leave that blank for now."

When they finished filling out the paperwork, Grace felt exhausted. She asked, "Do I just wear this hospital gown out of here?"

"Did you bring any other clothes?" As soon as the words escaped her mouth, Laura felt embarrassed. "I'm sorry, Grace. Of course, you didn't. We'll find something for you to wear."

She stood to leave but before she reached the door, she

turned toward Grace. “By the way,” she said. “The missing woman from two counties over ...”

“Yes?”

“Her name was Jane Landis, and her body was located and identified yesterday. So sad for the family.”

Deidra Wentworth

"Brynn has done a marvelous job," Deidra exclaimed. "I love the drapes. And our bedroom is more than I could have imagined. Your sister is incredibly talented."

Vance smiled. "She's always been good at making something out of nothing."

Deidra wrapped her arms around Vance. "You just don't appreciate Brynn the way I do."

"That's probably true," he admitted, and then he turned and called for the housekeeper, "Susan!"

Susan Toll scurried into the informal living area from some unknown location in the large house. She wore her light blue and white uniform, her graying hair tied back in a messy bun.

"Bring us two glasses of wine," Vance ordered.

As the housekeeper headed toward the kitchen, she picked Vance's jacket up off the floor and his cap off the back of a chair. Shaking her head with irritation, she left the room.

"Wine, huh?" Deidra smiled.

"To celebrate. There's always something to celebrate," he told her.

They sat down on the white couch as Susan brought wine to them.

"To Brynn and her creative brain." Deidra lifted her glass, and they toasted.

Later that evening, as Susan was gathering her things for the day, she called Deidra into the kitchen.

"Listen, Miss Wentworth," she said. "I agreed to stay on as your housekeeper after your parents died. But you need to let Mr. Montgomery understand that I am not his servant. I will not be ordered around by a privileged young know-it-all."

Deidra was taken by surprise. "I'm sorry, Susan. I didn't realize."

"Oh, here you are," Vance strutted into the room. "Susan, would you prepare my breakfast tonight? I have to get to the office extra early tomorrow." He floated out of the kitchen.

Susan scowled at Deidra, a deep crease between her glaring eyes.

~

Deidra's pearl white Subaru BRZ pulled into the parking lot at the Quinley Park Village Mall. She, Brynn, and India had declared the afternoon "girls' time." They pranced into Nordstrom and strode through Neiman-Marcus, making suggestions as to what the others should buy. As Deidra stood before the elegantly lit three-way mirror in a J. Crew tie-front top and white denims, Brynn nudged her.

"Girls, did you see that woman who just left the fitting room? Her clothes look like she shops at Old Lady Thrift Store."

The three of them giggled.

"We're terrible," observed India. "But you are funny, Brynn."

Having purchased the outfit, Deidra gasped when she noticed a beach bag hanging from the rack.

"Look at this," she exclaimed. "This is exactly what I've been wanting."

It was a Gucci canvas rope beach bag. Especially taken by the green and red stripes along the top, Deidra hung it from her shoulder. She modeled it for the others.

"Do I look chic?"

"Definitely," Brynn assured.

Deidra glanced at the price tag.

"Well, how much is it?" India asked.

"Three hundred ninety-five dollars," Deidra whispered.

"Are you going to get it?" asked India.

"Get it," Brynn encouraged. "You deserve something fun after all you've been through."

"I do," agreed Deidra. "Let's check out, then go for ice cream."

The women made their way to the Dairy Factory Ice Cream Parlor, where they sat around a small white table with triple-dip sundaes covered with fruit and whipped cream.

"Let's pretend this is healthy," India suggested. "After all, it contains milk and fruit, two parts of a healthy diet."

"Sounds reasonable to me," said Deidra.

"Tell me, what's it like living with my brother?" Brynn asked.

Deidra had just taken a huge bite of sundae. Before she could answer, Brynn said, "Don't respond; I know what it's like."

~

It was almost dark when Deidra came into her home through the garage door. She dropped her bags and hung up her jacket.

"Where were you?" Vance's voice echoed through the halls.

As she entered the kitchen, she found him pacing like a nervous tiger. "I've been waiting hours for you," he shouted.

Shocked, Deidra asked, "Why?"

"I had no idea where you were."

"Since when do you get to approve my schedule? I'll have you know that before I agreed to let you move in, I was an independent person, and I plan to stay that way."

Vance ran his fingers through his perfectly placed auburn hair.

"It's just that ..." He took a calming breath. "I had Susan prepare a meal for us. I thought we could have a romantic dinner together."

"Tonight?"

"Yes, tonight. I wanted to surprise you."

He led her through the kitchen to the formal dining room. Two complete place settings adorned one end of the long table. Between them stood a pair of taper candles which had obviously been burning awhile. Angry as Deidra was about Vance's assumption, she was touched by his thoughtful plan.

"If I had only known, I wouldn't have had the triple-dip sundae at Dairy Factory," she said.

"Dairy Factory?"

"Brynn and India. Girl time."

"Oh. Well, could you eat some beef tips with mushroom sauce?"

Deidra flashed a flirtatious look and said, "I'm willing to give it a try."

Vance pulled out her chair and then returned to the kitchen to retrieve the plates from the warmer. "It feels plenty warm yet." He arranged the dishes on the table. "For dessert, we have fresh fruit with whipped cream."

"Dessert?" Deidra sighed. "There is no way I can eat dessert."

"Maybe tomorrow?" he suggested.

"Tomorrow will be great."

Deidra sat at her desk, a pile of work stacked beside her. She thumbed through the top folder and tossed it aside for the next. Returning from a lengthy and stressful absence was harder than she expected.

"Good morning." In leaned Arthur Wexler.

"Hi, Arthur."

"You don't sound very enthusiastic," he commented.

She sighed. "Look at all this work," she exclaimed. "How will I possibly get through it all?"

He perched on the edge of her desk. "You'll get through

it one piece at a time. Do a little now, then take a break. Do a little more, and so on. I'd be glad to help out if I can."

"Thank you, but I don't know how you can. You have your own work."

"Take a little home with you tonight," he suggested. "You can work in front of the fireplace in the peace and quiet of your newly decorated home office. Maybe you'll run across the next great American novel."

"Anything less, and I'll fall asleep," she predicted. "Quiet evenings are harder to find at home these days."

He gave her an inquiring look.

"I told you that Vance is living with me now?"

Arthur nodded his head. "Tell me about Vance."

"We've known each other since college. I knew his sister in high school, so he's been around a long time. We hit it off and have dated off and on since college graduation. He's a nice guy, but ..."

"But?"

"But sometimes he's just in the way. The other day I went shopping with friends. We had a great time. When I returned home, Vance was irate because I hadn't told him where I was."

"Did he hurt you?"

"Oh no," Deidra assured her colleague. "He had supper ready for me, but he never told me about his plans. How was I supposed to know? But on top of that, I don't need to report my every move to him."

"Do you love this guy?" Arthur asked directly.

She thought about it. "I like him. He's fun. He's nice most of the time. He's someone to do things with. I don't know, Arthur. Sometimes I wonder if I'd be better off without him."

Arthur stood and turned to leave her office. "Time will tell, Deidra," he said on his way out the door.

Exhausted when she arrived home, Deidra kicked off her shoes and changed into yoga pants and an oversized t-shirt. She grabbed a water bottle from the refrigerator and made herself comfortable in front of the wall-sized television in the living area.

Vance hurried into the room, stopping short when he saw her.

"You're home," he exclaimed. "I didn't hear you come in." He leaned down and gave her a gentle kiss. "Why are you wearing that?" he asked.

"Why not? I'm exhausted and want to be comfortable when I dive into my pile of work tonight."

"You can't work tonight," he said. "My parents are coming over."

"What?" She jumped up. "Why are your parents coming?"

"Two reasons," Vance explained. "First, they want to see me. I'm their son, in case you've forgotten. Second, they want to see what Brynn has done with the house."

"Probably want to see how I've destroyed the house," Deidra grumbled.

"Stop," he said. "My parents don't dislike you that much."

Susan Toll stepped into the room and cleared her throat. "I left a pastry on the countertop. Is there anything else before I leave?"

"Thank you, Susan," Deidra said.

"We could use some fresh iced tea," Vance suggested.

"Of course." Susan turned abruptly and went back toward the kitchen.

"Vance, I have more work than I can possibly get done. I absolutely have to work tonight."

"Just relax," he told her. "You worked all day."

"Like you stop working the moment you step out of the office."

"That's different."

"How?" she asked.

"My job is more than a job, it's a …" He was interrupted by his cell phone. "Vance Montgomery," he answered as he slid into the next room.

Deidra stomped up the curvy stairway to change her clothes. "Why do I let him tell me what to do?" she scolded herself.

She pulled out a pair of jeans and a colorful Marina Rinaldi top. She went into her office, flopped down on the desk chair, and gazed at the pile of work she had brought home. As she reached for the top folder, she heard the door chime. Lawrence and Blaire Montgomery had arrived.

Lawrence was a tall man with a full head of well-manicured gray hair. He had a ready smile, which probably helped to make Montgomery Financial a success. He greeted Deidra with a fatherly half-hug.

Blaire Montgomery wore sleek black slacks and a green cashmere tunic vest. The color accentuated her copper, shoulder-length hair. She embraced Vance with a warm hug while glancing at Deidra out of the corner of her eye. Vance led his parents through the grand foyer, past the music hall, and into the library where they all found a seat on the cushiony, blue-velvet furniture.

"It's been a while since I've been in this house," Lawrence stated. "I had forgotten how lovely it is. Isn't that right, dear?"

"It's been a while, yes," Blaire said.

Deidra piped up, "Your daughter is so talented. Wait until you see how she decorated some of my rooms. I don't know what I would do without her."

"Would anyone like some iced tea?" Vance asked, trying to be a good host.

"How about some wine?" his mother suggested. "Do you have any wine?"

"I suppose so." He looked in Deidra's direction.

"Go down to the wine cellar," she said in a hushed voice. "The bottles on the bottom shelf of the north wall are what we want." Vance disappeared toward the wine cellar, leaving Deidra alone with his parents.

"I'm back to work now," she said, trying to initiate conversation.

"That's good," said Lawrence. "Now, remind me where you are employed?"

"I work at Alistair-Borne Publishing."

"Don't you remember, darling, when her daddy got that job for her after SMU?" Blaire said.

"I hope you are happy there," Lawrence said, smiling.

"I love it there," she confessed. "I am behind on work though, and even tonight, I have so much I need to get done."

"Don't let us stop you," Blaire spoke bluntly.

"I don't want to be rude," Deidra explained.

"Of course not," the older woman muttered.

When Vance entered with the wine tray, everyone relaxed a bit.

"Deidra was telling us how much work she has to do tonight," Blaire shared.

Vance gave his girlfriend a quick glare. "She is busy," he told them.

"How about you," Blaire addressed her son. "Is there anything you need? Anything at all?"

They were interrupted by Deidra's phone. "Excuse me." She walked to the corner of the library, checking the number as she went. No number appeared. She answered cautiously.

"I warned you," said the man on the other end. "Now, we need to make plans for you to hand over the money. I'll send you a blue envelope with details. No tricks, no cops. Got it?"

Flustered, Deidra hung up.

"Well, that was a one-sided conversation," Blaire said, laughing.

Vance recognized the pale look on Deidra's face. "Are you okay?" Clearly shaken, he helped her back to her chair. "Another crazy call?"

Deidra nodded. "A threat, Vance."

"Are you in trouble?" Blaire asked.

"Someone keeps making prank calls," she explained, "and I don't know what to do about it. It's very upsetting."

"Change your number," Lawrence suggested.

"But he knows where I live. I'm really scared."

"Do you think somebody wants to hurt you?" Lawrence set down his wine.

Deidra nodded, her lower lip trembling.

Lawrence Montgomery took a business card from his coat pocket and scribbled something on the back. Handing it to Deidra, he said, "If you need help, call this person. Lee Holland is a private investigator. I've used him for several business matters. Tell him I recommended him." He flashed Deidra his smile and gave her a quick, reassuring wink.

Grace Shepard

Laura Hoffman finished the paperwork in preparation for Grace's release from the hospital. "We're going to miss you," she said. The social worker popped up from her chair and pulled a cardboard box in from the hallway. "I did some shopping for you," she announced.

Grace looked curiously at her.

"I didn't think you'd want to enter Crestway Rehabilitation Center in a hospital gown."

Grace glanced down at herself. "Hospital gowns are the only thing I can remember wearing."

Laura thought about that as she scooted the box across for Grace to inspect. Inside were two pairs of jeans, several tops, pajamas, sweats, socks, underwear, and a bra.

"I guessed on the size, so you'll need to try them on."

Grace disappeared into the bathroom, coming out occasionally for advice on how to tie a top or adjust the bra. She finally came out wearing a slightly big pair of jeans and a Kansas City Chiefs t-shirt.

"Where did you get this stuff?" she asked.

"Walmart and the thrift store."

Grace looked at her with uncertainty.

"You'll get familiar with Walmart and the thrift store very soon, I'm sure. And there's one more thing," Laura said. From behind her chair, she pulled out a pair of walking shoes.

Grace slipped her feet into them and tied the laces. She walked across the room and back.

"These are so soft," she exclaimed.

"Memory foam."

"What?"

"Memory foam is what makes them so soft inside."

"I don't remember memory foam," said Grace. Both women laughed.

"Sounds like a good time in here," Dr. Milton entered the room. "Are you about ready for your departure, Grace?"

She shrugged.

"Crestway is a wonderful facility," he reassured her. "You will be safe and comfortable there."

"If you were my little sister," Laura said, "I would want you to go to Crestway."

"Are all the forms in order?" the doctor asked the social worker.

"All but a couple of blanks," she said. "They need to know how old Grace is."

The doctor smiled at Grace, who looked on with anticipation.

"I've determined you to be between twenty-eight and thirty-three. What's your pick, Grace?"

"I'll pick twenty-nine," she said.

The doctor laughed. "Doesn't every woman want to be twenty-nine? My wife has turned twenty-nine repeatedly."

Laura laughed out loud, while Grace appeared confused.

"We also need a birthday," Laura said.

"I have no idea," Grace said, sighing. "What day did I come out of my coma?"

"You came out of the coma gradually," the doctor said. "I believe the first day you became aware of others was July 8."

"Then let's make July 8 my birthday."

"Okay," Dr. Milton said. He scooted a chair near the bed where Grace was perched. "You've been through a lot. You may never know who you were before the accident. But I believe you can live a productive life from here. Mrs. Hoffman is familiar with many resources. Call her anytime you need to. Also, Dr. Yates could be a great help in coming to terms with building a new life."

"Thank you," Grace whispered. Dr. Milton stood and gave her a quick squeeze on her shoulder.

With all paperwork completed and Grace's few belongings dropped into the box, Dr. Milton said with a sparkle in his eye, "There's something I want to show you before you leave."

He and Laura led Grace down the hall, onto the elevator, and into a conference room.

"Surprise!" She was welcomed with a chorus of good cheer. The room, decorated with streamers and balloons, was swarming with people. The staff from ICU and some from her hallway gathered to celebrate her leaving. A large sheet cake was arranged in the center of a table with colorful napkins and forks. A punch bowl was filled with red juice. Cutting the cake was Adelle Hall, with her biggest smile yet.

"Get over here, baby girl," she called.

Adelle wrapped her arm around Grace's waist and said to the crowd, "This lady represents what St. Rafael is all about. We've watched her move from an unresponsive victim to a beautiful, more independent individual. We are so happy we got to meet you, Grace Shepard." Adelle's eyes filled with tears as she placed a delicately carved wooden cross around Grace's neck. "This cross is a symbol of something greater than yourself. Wherever you go from here, know that you are always loved. You are our Amazing Grace."

Everyone cheered.

~

Grace stepped through the hospital doors and slid into the passenger side of Laura Hoffman's car. The light almost blinded her.

"Are you ready for your next adventure?" Laura asked.

As they drove away from the hospital and through the commercial neighborhood, Grace was struck by the colors and shapes of buildings, the variety of plants, and the many people walking the sidewalks or waiting to cross the street.

"It smells different out here," Grace said. "The only smell I remember is hospital smell."

Laura pointed out landmarks such as McDonald's, Arby's, and a bank. "Do you remember what a bank is?" she asked Grace.

"A bank? It has to do with money, I think."

"That's right. Do you remember being in a bank?"

Grace thought. "Nothing comes to mind."

Eventually, they pulled into the circle drive of Crestway Rehabilitation Center. The one-story building was topped with a red-tile roof, and three brick pillars decorated the entrance. Laura helped Grace out of the car and walked with her through the sliding glass doors. A large circular desk dominated the reception area. Laura ushered Grace to a window labeled "Admissions."

A woman with bright red hair looked up from her paperwork and smiled. "Hello. We don't get a lot of patients who are able to walk in on their own."

"I'm working on it," Grace said quietly.

When paperwork was completed, Laura bid Grace goodbye. A nurse's aide picked up the box with Grace's belongings, held out her arm, and led the young woman down the shiny hallway to room number 8.

"This will be your room," she said. "You have a nice view of the park across the street." She placed the box on the chest of drawers and pulled open the blinds.

The room looked comfortable. A yellow spread decorated the bed. There were two recliners in front of a television and the chest of drawers. Along one wall was a narrow closet and a full bathroom.

"We want you to feel contented here," said the nurse aide. "You're welcome to bring anything that reminds you of home."

Grace thought that would be lovely, if only she could remember her home. It didn't take long to put her small wardrobe in the drawers and place the hairbrush, comb, and toothpaste she had received at the hospital on the bathroom counter. She sat on the bed, testing out its firmness.

She was about to make her way to a recliner when she was interrupted by a cheery, "Hello, there!"

Entering her room was a woman dressed in turquoise scrubs with pictures of poodles on them. Her brown hair, highlighted with blonde, hung loose around her shoulders. Red lipstick accentuated her smile.

"I'm Jess Flynn," she stated. "You must be Grace Shepard. I'm so excited about working with you." She helped Grace ease into the recliner and then took her place in the opposite chair. "I'm your occupational therapist. We will spend a lot of time together. Are you unpacked already?"

Grace nodded.

"Why, look at that," Jess exclaimed, pointing to the Kansas City Chiefs shirt Grace was wearing. "I have that same shirt. We could be twins." she laughed. "Of course, I'm quite a bit older than you, and my hips are much wider, but other than that."

Jess reviewed Grace's daily schedule for rehabilitation. It included group and individual counseling, time in the rehab gym, computer therapy, and eventually time in the Activities of Daily Living apartment. With warm enthusiasm, Jess offered Grace a wheelchair and took her on a tour of Crestway. Grace was quite impressed, although she had nothing to compare the rehab center to.

She joined a small group consisting of four other patients. Each had experienced brain trauma. A teenage girl, Emma, had been in a motorcycle accident on her way to prom. Bonnie, an older woman, recently suffered a stroke. Bill hurt himself when falling from a ladder, and Tyler experienced drug-induced brain damage at age twenty-three. Amanda, the facilitator of the group, came across as open and relaxed.

"Nobody is here to be judged. We are a team, working together to help each other heal," she told the group.

Grace did not know if she had ever met people this broken before, but their stories moved her heart. Emma had lost her boyfriend in the motorcycle wreck. Bonnie struggled to speak coherently. Bill had yet to find out if he would ever walk again, and Tyler's self-destructive behavior had regressed his brain function to that of a twelve-year-old.

"What brings you here, Grace?" Amanda asked as they went around the circle introducing themselves.

"I was in a car accident. When I woke up, I had no memory of who I was or where I was from."

"How long did it take to remember?" Bill asked.

"I haven't. Dr. Milton says I may never remember."

"What about your family?" Tyler asked. "Can they help you?"

"If I have family, I don't know who or where they are. I'm alone."

For the first time since Grace had come out of the coma, she broke down in tears. The group member on either side of her reached out and patted her back. Amanda paused to let her cry as long and as hard as she needed.

The therapy gym proved less emotional. Grace discovered how difficult it was to move and control her body. She practiced raising her arms and legs. Balance was the greater challenge. Jess worked with her in computer therapy, which dealt with fine motor skills and eye-hand coordination. They spent hours working with manipulatives, piecing puzzles, and playing mind games to practice sequencing and logic skills.

Grace grew to enjoy mealtimes in the dining hall. She often sat with members from her small group. She learned a lot about the world by listening to them. One day after lunch, Emma sat down at the piano in the dining hall and plucked out a simple tune.

"What are you playing?" Grace asked.

Emma gave her a strange look. "It's called 'Twinkle, Twinkle, Little Star.' Everybody knows that."

Grace laughed. "The tune I know, but the name was gone. Sing it to me."

Rather self-consciously, Emma sang the words, and soon Grace was able to join in. Grace slid onto the piano bench and placed her fingers on the keyboard. Without hesitation, her fingers sprang into action. They danced from key to key. Out poured a gorgeous and complicated classical piece. People stopped mid-sentence to listen. When she finished, the dining hall erupted in applause.

Jess came trotting over. "I didn't know you could play the piano."

"Neither did I," Grace admitted.

"What piece was that?"

Grace shrugged until someone in the hallway leaned in and said, "'Water Music Suite Number 2' by Handel."

"Those fingers can still work," Jess announced. "They work beautifully."

~

During her visits with Dr. Yates, Grace explored her grief. "It's not that I miss whatever I had," she expressed. "It's that I keep discovering how much I do not have now."

Dr. Ted listened intently, his white hair pulled into a ponytail and his smile reassuring. "Such as ..."

"Family, a hometown, friends from childhood, education. I have no idea if I have an education. I don't have a car, nor a driver's license, for that matter. I know how to use a computer but no clue how I learned. I can play the piano, but I remember no lessons or performances. Did I have a boyfriend? Is he worried sick about me?"

Dr. Ted leaned back in his chair. "Grace," he said. "If you are willing, we could try hypnosis on you. It sometimes helps uncover deep, forgotten experiences. I don't know if it will work in your case."

"Hypnosis?" she repeated the word.

"It's really an exercise in deep relaxation. Hypnosis is a tool for tapping into the subconscious mind."

"Sure," she said. "I'm willing." After a pause, she asked, "It won't hurt, will it?"

The doctor chuckled and reassured her that there would be no pain.

"That's one thing I do know about myself," she stated. "I hate pain."

Jess and Grace sat at a small table in the game room, playing rummy. Grace dealt the cards.

"So how did the hypnosis go?" Jess asked.

"It was relaxing," Grace said, sighing, "but it didn't

reveal anything new. Dr. Ted says that my experiences no longer exist in my brain."

"I was hoping it might answer some of your questions. So it's like starting with a fresh slate," Jess told her.

"What will I do from here?" Grace asked.

Jess stopped midway through her turn. "Grace, you are getting stronger every day. You are missing a lot of cognitive information, but you are a very bright person. You can learn anything you set your mind to. On top of that, you have many talents. Your keyboard skills are great, you play the piano beautifully, and your rummy game is getting better and better." She laughed.

"So when I leave here, where will I go?" Grace inquired.

"Wherever you choose," Jess said. "It must be your decision. There are a couple of board-and-care facilities in the area. A women's shelter might be another option. We may find you an assisted living situation."

Grace wondered how she was going to decide.

Grace spent two months at Crestway. She grew to appreciate the people she met at the rehab center, her small group, her caregivers, and especially Jess Flynn. Her occupational therapist walked the park with her, took her to McDonald's, and accompanied her on a shopping trip to the Dollar Mart. In the Activities in Daily Living apartment, Jess taught Grace how to cook and clean house. They did laundry together.

"This is the stuff of which life is made," Jess teased as they folded towels together.

Grace had no memory of laundry, cooking, or

housecleaning. She did remember how to write out a check, how to count change, and how to use a cell phone.

"It's funny the things I can do," Grace pointed out.

"Maybe you were never taught to cook," Jess suggested. "Some people aren't. Then there are people like my son. I tried to teach him to cook, but he apparently didn't have the aptitude for it."

"Where is your son?" Grace asked.

"Jarod is in California. He's making a good living, but I miss him being closer. He's one of those kids who left home and rarely returns."

"Do you have a husband?"

Jess shook her head. "Jarod's father and I divorced when he was about seven. I never heard from him again, except through child support checks. Sometimes I fear Jarod will look him up. I just don't want him to be disappointed."

"Are you lonely?" Grace felt concern for Jess.

"Sometimes," Jess admitted. "But I love the people I work with. I keep telling myself maybe someday I'll meet the real Mr. Right. In the meantime, I try to lose weight and experiment with my hair."

"At least you have hair," Grace pointed out.

"Your hair is coming back nicely. It's soft and brown and filling in quite well."

"I look like a boy," she replied, laughing. "It's all wispy and spiky."

Jess looked directly at Grace. "You, my friend, are a beautiful woman."

Arrangements were made for Grace to move into an assisted living facility. She was assigned a caseworker to help manage her needs. With tears in her eyes, she packed her box of belongings and said goodbye to the people she had grown close to.

Saturday, before she was to leave, many of the staff and residents gathered in the dining area. To her surprise, several of her original therapy group returned to greet her. Emma thanked her for a few piano lessons. Tyler promised that he would make better choices in the future. Bonnie arrived with her walker and said with crystal clear enunciation, "Best of luck, my dear."

Just as the nurse's aide pulled out her car keys to transport Grace, in ran Jess, completely out of breath.

"Jess!" Grace shouted. "I didn't think you would be here. It's Saturday."

Jess threw her arms around Grace. "I had to come."

"To see me off?"

"No. To take you home with me."

Grace was perplexed.

"Grace, we are two lonely people who need a family. If it's okay with you, I think we should be family for each other."

Deidra Wentworth

The candle on the table brightened the red-and-white checkered tablecloth. An Italian crooner sang softly in the background. Plates piled high with pasta, sauce, and cheese still sizzled before Deidra and Vance.

"This is what we both need, a little Italian," Vance proclaimed. "Pasta, cheese, and wine." He proceeded to fill both wine glasses.

"India is Italian." Deidra dug her teeth into a garlic breadstick. "It seems strange," she continued, "that people from Italy would name their daughter India."

"Kind of like Asian parents naming their child José." They both laughed.

"People are strange, you know," she reflected.

Vance grinned. "Don't forget, Dee, you are talking to the offspring of Lawrence and Blaire Montgomery. I know strange."

"As does the daughter of Sterling and Patricia Wentworth."

"But look at us," he said. "We turned out great, don't you think?"

Deidra smiled and took a sip of wine.

Vance reached out and touched her arm.

"It's nice to see you relaxed tonight," he said.

"I am so glad that I had my phone number changed. That was your dad's idea. It was a good one," she pointed out.

Just then a text message sounded on Deidra's phone.

"Weren't you the one who made me silence my phone tonight?" Vance protested.

Deidra reached for her phone. "India must have known we were talking about her," she said.

"Or my sister," Vance added.

As she glanced at her message, Deidra's complexion changed from rosy to pale.

"Are you okay?"

"We need to get out of here."

"What? What is it?"

She handed him her phone to read the message. Printed in bold letters he read, "I can see you now. You cannot hide. Tell me where and when we can meet up. It's time to pay your debt."

They glanced around, when suddenly, a deep, scratchy voice spoke her name, and she jumped.

A hand rested on her shoulder. "I didn't mean to frighten you."

Turning, she saw the humble face of Arthur Wexler.

"Arthur," she gasped. "I'm not used to seeing you outside the office."

"I hope you're having a nice evening," he said, smiling weakly.

"Arthur, I'd like you to meet my boyfriend, Vance Montgomery."

The two men shook hands rapidly. Seeing Arthur and Vance together felt strange to Deidra, as she watched her work life and home life collide.

"Nice to meet you," Arthur said quickly. "I believe I'm being seated. Better run."

Vance studied Arthur as he plodded toward a corner table. "Maybe he's your stalker," he whispered.

"Arthur?" Deidra exclaimed. "No way. He's a nice guy. Very nerdy, but nice."

"Look at him, Dee. Those narrow eyes and that hair combed down over his receding hairline."

"Vance, stop."

"Think about it. He knows you. He knows where you live. He knows where you work. Did you give him your new phone number?"

Struck with fear and anger, Deidra ordered, "We're out of here, Vance. Get some take-out boxes. I'm going to the car." She started to leave but then thought twice. "Hurry," she said in a panicked voice. "Somebody is watching me. I don't believe it's Arthur, but it is somebody."

Safe in her house, Deidra and Vance picked at their take-out meal while seated at the breakfast bar.

"This didn't turn out to be the night I planned," Vance said, scanning his phone for messages.

"I changed my number, but that didn't help," Deidra sighed. "What am I supposed to do now? Do I deliver what he wants? Meet him in some eerie location? Do I risk being murdered?"

Vance wrapped his arm around her shoulders. "Do you remember the other thing Dad suggested?"

Deidra thought for a moment. "The private investigator?"

"It's the next step, Dee."

Deidra rested her head on Vance's shoulder. "I can't live like this anymore. I'm going to call him."

"First thing in the morning," he said. "And maybe you should stay away from work. I don't trust that Wexler guy."

Deidra rolled her eyes. "Arthur Wexler is as innocent as they come. I could believe he's a virgin, but not a threat."

Deidra and Vance stepped into the office of Lee Holland, private investigator. The room was subtlety lit by a desk lamp and soft daylight stretching in through the window. When Holland took his seat behind the desk, he appeared as a silhouette in front of the window. His large metal desk was piled high with stacks of papers, folders, envelopes, and sticky notes. A shabby basket in one corner of the desk overflowed with flash drives, each labeled with a series of letters and numbers.

Holland presented a professional appearance, wearing a suit and striped tie. His brown hair was cut short, and his glasses blended well into his features.

"I've worked with your father on a couple of occasions, Mr. Montgomery. I have great respect for him," the investigator said.

Switching tasks, Holland presented a Terms of Services Agreement. Line by line, he explained process and expectations for the investigator/client agreement. He stated his fee and offered to set up a payment schedule.

"Money's no issue for Deidra," Vance said.

She gave him a sharp glance before signing the agreement.

Deidra described her situation, the threats, the fear, and her confusion about how to handle it.

Holland listened carefully and then said, "A legitimate lender would use a collection agency, not a series of threats. How much is he asking for?"

Deidra told him the figure.

"That's no petty loan," the investigator stated.

"I've changed my phone number, but he can still contact me. I'm sure he knows where I live."

"Do you have a security system in the home?"

"Absolutely."

"Have it set at all times."

"Should I go to work?"

"Keep your day as normal as you can, but do not go any place you will be alone. Don't even take out the trash alone."

"I never take out the trash," Deidra said. "That's Susan's job."

Holland raised his eyebrows in question.

"She's my housekeeper," Deidra explained. "My parents hired her years ago."

The investigator turned to his computer and quickly typed out a lengthy list. He grabbed the paper from the printer and handed it to Deidra.

"This is a list of items I need from you. The more you can provide, the better chance I have of uncovering whatever we're dealing with. Do you have your father's cell phone?"

Deidra shook her head. "It was destroyed in the crash."

She examined the lengthy list.

"If you could provide me with a roster of your father's business contacts, ledgers, financial statements; any of that would be helpful. A phone log, if possible, or access to his email accounts. See if you can find a list of passwords he may have used. Most people have them saved somewhere where they can access them easily. Files related to Dehlco Petroleum and any files with unrecognizable labels could be useful."

"I feel like I'm spying on my dead father," Deidra said.

"Your father has no use of these things anymore. You, on the other hand, need them for your own safety."

~

It felt like a scavenger hunt when India and Brynn joined Deidra and Vance in searching the house for possible evidence. They started in her father's office. Except for dust, the room remained as he left it. The file cabinet was locked, so they swarmed the desk. Vance removed every desk drawer for easy access.

"A key," Brynn exclaimed. It fit the file cabinet. "What exactly am I supposed to look for?"

Deidra handed her the list of objects.

"This looks like a ledger," Vance announced.

He and Deidra thumbed through the book of expenses and deposits. "Put it in the box for Holland," Deidra said.

India gathered all the flash drives they found and dropped them in the box.

"Look at this," Brynn proclaimed. "It's your college tuition records, Deidra. Didn't he ever throw anything away?" She pulled out another file containing a directory from Dehlco Petroleum. "This might be helpful."

"Drop it in the box," Deidra instructed.

Vance tried to access Sterling Wentworth's laptop computer. "Any idea what his password was?"

"I never cared what his password was," Deidra said.

"Birthday, anniversary, high school jersey number?"

"No idea."

Deidra set aside any scrap with a telephone number on it. Several mysterious file folders were pulled. One by one, they replaced the desk drawers, until the last one, which Deidre struggled to slide in.

"This one won't slide in." She struggled with the heavy drawer.

"Let me get it," Vance offered.

"I tell you it won't slide. Something is in the way."

Deidra set the drawer down and felt inside the open space. An object was hanging down from the drawer above. She pulled, and out came an envelope.

"Here's the problem," she said. Opening the envelope, she discovered several three-by-five index cards. In her father's handwriting was a list of numbers, letters, and symbols.

"Those are passwords," Brynn exclaimed.

Vance grabbed the cards from her and slid in behind the computer. He typed the first password. Nothing. He typed the second. "Bingo! I got into his computer."

While Vance worked in the office, Deidra, Brynn, and India went upstairs to the room her parent's bedroom furniture had been moved to. Unarranged, and cluttered, they checked out the chest of drawers and the dresser.

"Look at this." Brynn held up a pair of bright yellow socks. "Did Sterling Wentworth wear these?"

Deidra snickered. "A gag gift from his secretary."

India picked up a framed family photo from the dresser. "This was a while back."

In the photo, Deidra was dressed in her high school band uniform as she stood behind her parents.

"Don't look at that," Deidra objected, studying the photo herself. "I gave Dad that tie for Christmas, so he wore it for the picture. But that dress Mom is wearing is one I never liked. She probably wore it to irritate me."

"Deidra," India scolded. "Your mother was a lovely person. She wouldn't do that."

"She would."

"Only because the two of you were so much alike that you sometimes annoyed one another."

Deidra continued to study the photograph.

"Oh, Deidra," India whispered, "you have lost so much."

Returning the photo to its place, a business card fluttered out from behind the frame. Brynn picked it up.

"It's a phone number," she said. "Do you recognize it, Deidra?"

"I've never seen it before. It could be important. We'll put it in the box."

They entered the closet where Deidra had haphazardly hung her parents' clothing. They checked pockets and handbags for any small items of interest. Behind her father's many suits, Deidra uncovered an expandable leather attaché briefcase with a combination lock. She pulled it out.

"Great," she grumbled. "It's locked."

"Take the whole case to Lee Holland," Brynn suggested. "He should know how to get into it. I'll take it downstairs."

Brynn and India left to add the attaché to the pile of possible evidence. Deidra sat down on the stripped bed and glanced around the room. So many memories. Spotting the nightstand, she slid open the drawer. There, along with a flashlight and some anti-snoring strips, lay a Springfield XDM handgun. Deidra gently picked up the weapon. She ran her fingers along its shape and slid her index finger into the trigger. She aimed.

Grace Shepard

The Lakewood Villa Apartments offered a welcoming environment for Grace. Jess Flynn lived on the second floor of the east wing. The two-bedroom, two-bath apartment was ample room for both women. Grace settled into the room that had once belonged to Jess's son, Jarod. Still displaying a high school pennant and shelves of model airplanes, Grace sensed remnants of a teenage boy.

"Suppose Jarod comes home for a visit?" Grace inquired.

"He hasn't been home in four years, so I wouldn't worry," Jess assured her. "If he shows up, there are motels nearby. Feel free to make the room comfortable for you. I can store Jarod's things in a box."

"I haven't got much to unpack," Grace pointed out.

As Grace placed her clothes into the chest of drawers, she gently fingered the wooden cross that hung around her neck, recalling Adelle's reassuring words, "remember that wherever you go from here, you will always be loved."

Grace glanced into the mirror above the chest. *Who is that person staring back at me?* The reflection revealed a thin face with grey eyes. A scar ran down her right cheek and jaw. Short brown bangs reached halfway to her eyebrows.

Jess left for work every morning. Grace watched TV and often went for walks around the complex. She discovered the swimming pool in the outdoor court, the activity room, and the kitchen on the first floor of Lakewood Villa.

"Where is the lake?" Grace asked Jess when she returned.

"What?"

"The lake. You know, Lakewood."

Jess laughed. "Don't waste your time looking. There is a small man-made pond on the other side of the complex. It is visible from about four apartments. And as far as the wood, you've seen the cedar trees by the entrance, and there are a couple of oaks out by the pool."

"So 'Lakewood' is really a figment of somebody's imagination," Grace surmised.

"You got it," Jess agreed.

After a week, Grace began feeling guilty. Jess worked all day and then came home and fixed supper, while she sat around the apartment. "I need something to do," she said as Jess emptied the dishwasher. "I feel like I'm mooching."

"You shouldn't feel that way," Jess assured her. "I did the same chores when it was just me."

"What can I do to help?" Grace asked, reaching for the silverware basket.

Together they decided that Grace could act as housekeeper. She could dust the furniture and clean the floors. Twice a week, she would cook dinner.

"I will do my best," she promised, wiping her hand across a dusty shelf.

"We practiced in the rehab apartment, but if you have any questions, just ask. We'll work it out," Jess assured her.

~

Jess decided that it was time for Grace to have a shopping experience. One chilly day, they drove to the mall. Once inside, Grace recognized the purpose of her surroundings.

"Do you like JC Penney?" Jess asked.

"I have no idea who that is," she answered.

They entered the store and began to browse the ladies' department.

"Do you see anything you want to try on? It's time to think about winter clothes," Jess told her. "You'll need a coat as well."

Grace tried on several items including sweaters, slacks, tops, as well as jackets and coats. Somewhat overwhelmed, she settled on a couple of outfits, a pair of stylish boots, and a heavy parka.

Grace strained to read the tags. "What does this say?" she asked Jess.

"Now Grace," Jess said, "I know you can read."

"I can read fine," she replied. "I just can't see very well."

"In that case, I'll make you an appointment with an optometrist."

As they exited the fitting room, a cheery voice called out, "Jess! Jess Flynn."

"Mrs. Bellamy," Jess greeted a stocky older woman with curly grey hair.

"Grace, meet Mrs. Bellamy. She lives at Lakewood with us."

The older woman offered a welcoming smile. "Grace, is it?"

Grace nodded. "Grace Shepard."

"And how long have you lived at Lakewood?"

"Only a short while," she explained. "I'm staying with Jess."

"I'm Mrs. Bellamy. My name means 'beautiful friend.' I hope that's what I can be to you." She spoke rapidly with hardly a breath. "Won't you come to our next social? It's such fun when we all get together. Did you just move here? I detect a slight Southern accent. Where is home?"

Feeling unsure, Grace shot Jess a look of helplessness.

"We really must head on, Mrs. Bellamy," Jess said, stepping in. "We have a full schedule. See you soon." She steered Grace down the aisle and to the checkout line.

Entering Jess's car, Grace took a sigh of relief. "I had no idea what to say to that woman. Where is home?"

"Mrs. Bellamy is a nice person; she's a retired schoolteacher and is used to talking to everyone. Take some deep breaths and relax."

"Let me drive," Grace said.

"You want to drive?"

"It will give me a sense of control," Grace explained.

Jess hesitated and then said, "I'll let you drive around the lot, but you don't have a license to drive anywhere else."

They traded places, and Grace turned the key and started the car; she shifted into drive and went to the far end of the parking lot and then continued around the other side of the mall. Eventually, she pulled into a parking space.

She smiled and said, "That felt familiar."

~

By week's end, Jess sported a new hairstyle, with pinkish-red highlights, and Grace had a new pair of prescription glasses.

"This is the new us," Jess laughed as they left the optometrist shop.

Grace chuckled and then shook her head. "I don't know who the old me was. When we met Mrs. Bellamy at the mall, I felt like a childish fool."

"Why?"

"I couldn't even tell her where I grew up. I must have looked like a simpleton. What am I going to tell people?"

"Well," Jess said, "if we don't know your past, we'll have to make one up."

She pulled out a sheet of paper and placed it on the table.

"What are people most likely to ask?" Jess thought out loud. "Your name, for sure." On the paper, she wrote "Grace Shepard." "What about a middle name? Have you given any thought to that?"

"What's your middle name?" Grace asked.

"You don't want mine. It's Lynn."

It took a second before Grace asked, "Your name is Jessica Lynn Flynn?"

"That's me," Jess affirmed. "I rhyme. It is not my parents' fault. Flynn is my married name."

"What sounds good with Grace? And don't suggest Grace Leopard Shepard."

The women howled with laughter. They listed several options: Anne, Louise, Elizabeth. Finally, they agreed Grace Katherine sounded lovely.

"Now, where did you grow up?"

"The only place I know about is here, and I don't know much about Wichita," Grace pointed out.

"You grew up in Wichita." Jess wrote it down. "I'll take you on a drive to familiarize you with your hometown. Parents' names?"

"You know," Grace pondered, "The first people I remember are Dr. Dean Milton and Adelle Hall. My parents can be Dean and Adelle Shepard."

"Good idea. Where did you go to school?"

A blank look came over Grace.

Jess thought. "If you tell them one of the high schools in the city, someone will have gone there. You were homeschooled. Your mother was a teacher and homeschooled you."

"That works," Grace agreed. "And what did my father do for a living?"

"A doctor? A construction worker? An architect? A dentist?" suggested Jess.

"A dentist," Grace agreed, and Jess wrote it down.

"No siblings," Jess continued. "Both parents were killed in the car accident that left you with the scar on your face. It devastated you, so I invited you to come live with me."

"What about work experience?" Grace asked.

"You worked hard at Crestway Rehab. That's where we met. We worked together."

Grace smiled as Jess finished writing.

"Here's your story." Jess handed the paper to Grace. "Now, you need an opportunity to try it out."

~

The Fall Festival was an annual event for the residents of Lakewood Villa Apartments. When she entered the activity room, Grace was surprised by the attendance. She had no idea how many people lived in the complex. There were many young and middle-aged professionals, an assortment of retired folks, with a smattering of young couples. A man in his thirties greeted Jess and Grace at the door.

"Welcome to the Fall Festival," he said with a shy but genuine smile.

"Jeremy," Jess greeted. "I'd like you to meet my friend, Grace Shepard. She's living with me."

Jess turned to Grace. "Jeremy Barton lives down the hall from us."

"Nice to meet you," Grace said.

All at once, a loud voice shouted, "Folks, if I could have your attention!"

It was Mrs. Bellamy from the fitting room, who oversaw the Fall Festival because, as Jess said, if you want something done, put Mrs. Bellamy in charge. She gave directions for passing through the sloppy Joe, chips, and cookie line. Jess and Grace took their plates to one of the many round tables. It proved a great place for observing their neighbors. Jess pointed people out to Grace, filling her in on personalities and occupations. Mrs. Bellamy and Jeremy made their way to the table.

"Good to see you again, Grace," Mrs. Bellamy said.

Grace was surprised she remembered her name.

Mrs. Bellamy dominated the conversation, mainly by asking Grace questions. "Where did you say you were from?"

"I'm from here in Wichita," Grace said with as much confidence as she could muster. "My father was a dentist and my mother, a teacher."

That sparked the older woman's interest. "A teacher, you say. Where did she teach? What grade?"

"She taught all grades since she homeschooled me."

"Is that right? And your father; is he retired?"

Grace cleared her throat. "My parents were both killed in a car accident."

Mrs. Bellamy's mouth dropped opened.

"So sorry," Jeremy said quietly.

"It was the same accident that gave me this scar," Grace informed them.

"Grace is making a new start," Jess explained. "That's why I invited her to move in with me."

"Bless your heart," said Mrs. Bellamy.

"Good luck," Jeremy smiled. His eyes were sincere and sympathetic.

The evening progressed as everyone formed groups for a pumpkin-carving contest. Grace joined forces with Jess, Jeremy, and a recently retired couple. Together, they planned their design. When Jess accidentally carved a crooked smile, she handed the knife to Grace. Without thinking, Grace engraved a crazy mouth complete with fangs and a forked tongue.

"How did you learn to do that?" Jeremy inquired.

"I have no idea," Grace answered honestly.

By the end of the evening, Grace felt pleased that there

were several people in the complex she could now call by name.

~

Grace sat across from Dr. Ted in what was now a familiar, dimly lit room at Crestway Rehabilitation Center.

"Jess is helping me build an identity," she told the psychiatrist. "At least I will have a story to tell people."

"How do you feel about the story?" asked Dr. Ted, his frizzy gray hair resting on his shoulders.

"It gives me something to say, but I'm scared that someone will ask me a question I don't know the answer to."

"Would that be a problem?"

"I want to look confident, like I know what I'm talking about."

"That's a reasonable desire."

"Other than that," Grace continued, "I'm feeling like a burden. Jess is letting me pitch in with housework, but I need something to do. I need to have a reason to get up in the morning."

"And you can't work because ..." the doctor began, inviting her to elaborate.

"I don't know what experience I've had. I don't know what kind of education I have. I don't even know what my Social Security number is."

Dr. Ted stretched his long legs out as he leaned back in his chair. "As Grace Shepard you have no education and no experience, although I'm quite convinced that in your past life, you were well educated and experienced. That doesn't help you at this point."

"So what do I do? Enroll in high school?" she asked, laughing at the ridiculous idea.

"Not exactly, but I suggest you seek a Graduate Equivalent Degree, or GED. You may be surprised at how much you know when it comes to academics. That's the thing with complete declarative amnesia. The experiences of your past are gone, but the knowledge and skills are still in your brain."

"Do I need a Social Security number to enroll?"

"There are ways to get you fixed up with a legal identity," Dr. Ted said. "I'm going to contact David Edelman, an attorney who practices family law. He has also helped abused spouses who were living in fear create new identities. Mr. Edelman knows the law and what needs to be done for you to live legally as Grace Shepard."

Deidra Wentworth

Deidra scurried around her dressing room, trying to make up time lost after sleeping in. A quick tap on the door and Susan Toll calling, "Your mail is here," sent her to the bedroom door. A small pile of envelopes lay on the chair outside the room. Thumbing through the contents, she came to a small envelope with a handwritten address. She pulled out a one-page note.

"Time is up. Be careful. Consider this fair warning."

In a sudden panic, she called out, "Vance! Vance, come in here."

A shirtless Vance came out of the bathroom, talking on his phone. He held up a finger as if to say, "Wait."

"Look at this," she said, handing him the note.

After he ended his call, Vance glanced at the note. "What are you supposed to do?" he asked. "Do they want you to drop the money off somewhere? Maybe you should put an ad in the paper that a huge amount of money is available for whoever has been threatening Deidra Wentworth." He laughed at the ridiculous suggestion.

"That's not funny," she cried. "How am I supposed to live?" She paced the room. "I'm afraid to go anywhere. I cannot even drive to work alone. Somebody is apparently watching me all the time, and I have no idea who it is." She burst into tears.

"Just calm down." He reached for her arm. "Lee Holland is on the case. He's a good investigator."

"I hope so because I can't handle this much longer."

They heard movement in the hallway. Turning to check it out, they saw Susan scurrying past the open door.

"How much do you think she heard?" Vance asked.

"I think she hears everything," Deidra said.

Deidra sat with Vance in Lee Holland's office. Her foot tapped nervously.

"I have information for you," the investigator said. "Thanks to the telephone number you found on the business card, I was able to track some of your father's communication to a Reliant Loan Corporation."

"He did owe money?" Deidra asked.

Holland nodded, and said, "Lots of it."

Deidra felt confused. "What did he need money for? They owned the house, the plane, and Dehlco Petroleum is making large profits. I don't understand."

"Reliant Loan Corporation," explained Holland, "is a front for a loan shark."

"Why would Daddy go to a loan shark?"

The investigator cleared his throat. "Apparently Sterling

Wentworth did not want you or your mother to find out that he was neck-deep in gambling debts."

"Gambling debts!" Deidra was shocked. "How did he even know a loan shark? Vance, can you believe it?"

Vance shook his head quickly.

"A loan shark will set up anywhere people may be desperate; the tracks, casinos, stadiums," Holland explained. "I must warn you that a loan shark can be merciless. You must be cautious. Be careful about where you go, who you talk to, and try not to find yourself alone anywhere."

"Who is this loan shark? Do you have a name?"

"Not yet. It could be anyone, from a total stranger to somebody you see every day."

~

Armed with pepper spray and her father's handgun, Deidra waited in her driveway until Brynn arrived. Arrangements had been made for Brynn to follow her to Alistair-Borne Publishing House each morning and on her way home again after work. Driving alone would almost be as dangerous as taking public transportation. In Deidra's mind, everyone was a potential stalker.

"Let's roll," Brynn called out the car window.

Deidra gave her a thumbs up, and they moved down the curvy drive and into traffic. When they arrived at the publishing house, Brynn watched her friend park and then drove slowly beside her until she entered the building.

"See you tonight," Brynn said, waving goodbye.

Deidra focused straight ahead as she rode the elevator to the third floor and made her way to her office. She usually felt quite safe at work, but anymore she looked upon each person suspiciously.

Passing the receptionist's desk, Deidra gave a simple nod before disappearing into her small office. She locked the door behind her. There was something about reading and reviewing manuscripts that gave Deidra comfort. Maybe because it was a familiar activity, or maybe it was an escape from real life. Forty minutes into her day, the doorknob shook. Somebody was trying to enter her office.

"Deidra, are you in there?" It was Arthur Wexler, who usually popped in unannounced.

She quickly unlocked the door, and he stepped inside.

"Is your doorknob broken?" he asked, inspecting the apparatus.

"I must have locked it by mistake," she said.

Arthur perched on the corner of her desk. "Have you had a chance to review *Scream of Silence*? I'm anxious to hear your opinion." Arthur noticed that Deidra was staring out the window at the building next door.

"Deidra?" he spoke softly.

She shook to attention. "I'm sorry. What were you saying?"

"Are you okay?" he asked, concern in his eyes.

"Fine," she answered sharply.

"You don't look fine."

"I just haven't slept much lately," she explained.

"Why? Is it Vance?"

"No," she insisted. "It's not Vance."

"If he ever hurts you for any reason, he'll have me to answer to."

Deidra chuckled at the image of Arthur Wexler beating up Vance Montgomery. Not likely, she thought. For a fleeting moment, she thought about coming out with the truth. He seemed so caring and authentic. On second thought, Vance did not trust Arthur. What if he was the loan shark?

Ten minutes before Deidra was to leave work, her phone rang; it was Brynn.

"I am so sorry, but I'm tied up and won't be able to follow you home."

"Brynn! What if I'm kidnapped in the parking lot? I could be car-jacked at a traffic light." Deidra began to panic. "I need you to come."

"You know I would if I could. But work is crazy …"

Deidra sighed in resignation. "I know, Brynn. It's okay."

As she hung up the phone, Arthur popped his head in. "See you tomorrow," he said. "Have a good night."

"Wait," Deidra called. "I'm embarrassed to ask, but could you walk me to my car?"

A confused look crossed his face. "If you want me to," he said. "I'd be glad to."

Deidra grabbed her bag, and Arthur followed her to the parking lot. She was alert to every shadow and movement.

"Where are you parked?" he asked.

"Right over there," she said, pointing, and then she stopped suddenly.

"What is it?" he asked.

Approaching the Subaru BRZ, they saw it. All four tires had been slashed.

~

By the time the tow truck transported Deidra's car to the garage and installed four new tires, it was dark. Arthur waited with her, patient with her anxiety. A set of headlights raced into the garage lot. They heard the squeal of brakes and then saw Vance hop out of his car and rush into the garage's waiting area.

"Vance!" Deidra rushed to him in relief.

"Are you okay?" he asked.

"I'm fine."

Vance looked over at Arthur Wexler, sizing him up and down.

"It was quite the shock for her," Arthur reported.

"You can leave now," Vance told him.

"Vance, Arthur was a lifesaver. He called the tow truck and drove me over here," Deidra informed. "Thank you, Arthur."

~

Vance and Deidra snuggled in bed that night, glad to be safe at home together.

"Vance, I was so scared," Deidra confessed. "I thought someone would hop out and grab me."

"You're safe now," he said, kissing the top of her blonde hair.

"Arthur was so helpful."

"I don't trust him," Vance said.

"Are you jealous?" Deidra teased.

Vance laughed. "Jealous of Wexler? Never. He's an awkward geek."

"He's very kind."

They lay in silence for a spell until Vance sat up quickly.

"I have an idea," he announced. "I know what you need; what all of us need."

Deidra stared curiously at him.

"Let's have a party."

"A party?"

"Sure. We can call it a housewarming party. We'll invite friends over ..."

"Vance, I have no idea who is threatening me. They could show up at the party."

"No, Dee. We will only invite good friends. It will be in the safety of home with just us, Brynn, India, and a few more of our close friends," he explained.

"Arthur Wexler?" she teased.

"No. No Wexler. He belongs at your work, not your home." Vance drew her close and kissed her deeply. "You need some fun," he pointed out.

That, she could not dispute.

Grace Shepard

David Edelman, attorney-at-law, welcomed Grace and Jess with ease. Edelman was rather short and stocky. He wore an open-collared shirt rolled up on his forearms. His dark-framed glasses and neatly trimmed beard fit his face nicely. The three of them sat around a small table in his office.

"Can I get you coffee or a soda?" he asked.

"Coffee sounds great," Jess said. Grace requested a can of Coke.

Once everyone had their beverage, the attorney explained his understanding of Grace's request.

"According to Dr. Yates, you are seeking to establish a legal identity after losing all memory of who you were in the past."

"That's right," Grace affirmed. "At this point, I feel like a nameless entity."

"We can't have that," Edelman said, smiling. "I've

assisted others in establishing new identities. Many people just want a name change, but there are occasions when an abused spouse seeks a new identity for safety reasons. The ability to hide from harm and start fresh warranted the action."

"So, a new identity for Grace is legally possible?" Jess asked.

"Certainly. But it can be a lengthy process. What you need the most is patience."

"How long will it take?" Grace asked.

"Let me explain the process." The attorney presented a sheet of paper listing every step necessary. "First, we will need to develop facts, name, date of birth, that sort of thing. Then you will need to petition to the State of Kansas. There will be a name change hearing before a judge. You will also need to apply for a new Social Security number and photo ID, such as a driver's license. There will be times when all we can do is wait. Government agencies never seem to share the expedient expectations that most applicants have. Any questions?"

Grace had more questions than she could think of. Her mouth dropped open.

Edelman smiled. "Don't worry. We will do it one step at a time."

They started with basic information. Name? Grace Katherine Shepard. Date of birth? July 8. Age? Twenty-nine. Reason for change?

"Do I say I have total declarative amnesia and remember nothing of my past?"

"Who made that diagnosis?" Edelman asked.

"It was Dr. Dean Milton."

"We will write down the diagnosis, then we can attach

an affidavit from Dr. Milton, stating your diagnosis and his prognosis."

By the time they left Edelman's office, Grace felt like she had taken the first step to becoming a legitimate person.

With determination, Grace began studying for her Graduate Equivalency Degree. She ordered a book entitled *GED Preparation* and studied every moment she had.

"I think I can do the English and grammar part without much trouble. Math and history may be an issue. Wouldn't you think I'd remember what I once learned?" she asked Jess one evening.

"Could be you never learned much about those subjects. I have a master's in occupational therapy but wouldn't be able to answer many of the questions in that book." She placed a bowl of popcorn between them. "Read me a question," Jess suggested.

Grace read, "The rate of a chemical reaction depends on all of the following except?"

"What are the choices?" Jess asked. "Is it multiple choice?"

"Amount of mass lost. Surface area. Temperature. Presence of catalysts." Grace looked up to see the blank expression on Jess's face.

"Give me a moment," Jess said, struggling to come up with the answer. Finally, she admitted, "I don't know. It's been too long since I've studied this stuff. Remember, there are always online classes you could take."

On the day of the hearing, Grace dressed in a casual skirt and blouse, taking Jess's suggestion to appear somewhere between uppity and downtrodden. David Edelman drove her to the Sedgwick County Courthouse. It was a large, blue building stretching about ten stories high. After they entered the doorway, they were greeted by a security guard. Purses, bags, cell phones, and keys were placed in a bucket for scanning. Edelman casually walked through a metal detector, so Grace followed. After reclaiming their belongings, they stepped into an elevator crammed with people. Some wore suits, some wore ragged jeans and t-shirts. Edelman led the way through the crowded space. He knew exactly where to go.

"Just relax," he told Grace. "We will be meeting in the judge's chambers, not a courtroom."

That bit of information did relieve some of the anxiety Grace was feeling.

They walked down a hallway that was practically empty. Only a few voices echoed through the corridor. They entered a room where Edelman was greeted by a black woman wearing a dark robe.

"Good to see you, Mr. Edelman," she said warmly.

"Grace, this is Judge Diane Holmes."

The room smelled of polish. Wooden panels and bookshelves lined the space. A large dark walnut desk was positioned at one end of the room. An assortment of plush chairs and a couch faced the desk.

"Grace, how are you?" a male voice spoke. It was Dr. Milton.

Excited to see the doctor, she held back from embracing him. "I'm doing well," she said, smiling.

At the judge's command, everyone took a seat.

"I have your petition for a name change," said Judge Holmes. "What a tragic situation you find yourself in," she offered. "You remember nothing before the accident?"

"No, Your Honor. I remember nothing."

Dr. Milton spoke up. "What Grace is experiencing is ..."

"And you are ...?" the judge interrupted.

"I'm Dr. Dean Milton. I was Grace's neurological surgeon. You should have an affidavit from me."

Judge Holmes pulled a paper from the folder before her. "Yes, I see. And what is it you would like to say?"

"Total declarative amnesia is an exceedingly rare condition," the doctor explained. "Grace retains many of the skills she had before. However, she has no experiential memory. That part of her brain is gone. She has no recall of who she was before."

"I see your predicament," the judge said. She studied the petition before her and Dr. Milton's affidavit. "Did she have any identification when she was first brought into St. Rafael?"

"None," spoke the doctor.

Silence filled the room as Grace grew increasingly anxious.

Judge Holmes gave a deep sigh, then spoke. "Hundreds of thousands of people are reported missing each year. Many more go unreported. You are probably one of them. My concern is that someday your identity will be uncovered. What would you do then?"

Edelman cleared his throat to speak. "Your Honor, I understand your concern. I think we all wonder the same thing. But without a legal identity, Grace has no Social Security number and therefore cannot be employed. She has no identification card, no driver's license. Without a legal identity, she cannot enroll in an educational program. We are asking you to grant her an opportunity to live a life after that dreadful accident."

"Thank you, Mr. Edelman." Judge Holmes looked at Grace and broke into a smile. "You are a brave woman," she said. "You deserve a second chance at life."

Moving over to her desk, the judge proceeded to sign several papers. "Grace Katherine Shepard," she said. "You will receive your legal document in the mail. As of this moment, you have a name, you have a date of birth, and they will be on record at the Kansas Office of Vital Statistics. Good luck on your journey. What will be your next step?"

Grace could not help but grin. "I will apply for a Social Security number and take the GED test as soon as possible."

In celebration of her legal identity, Jess took Grace out for supper.

"Where do you want to go?" Jess asked as they buckled into the car.

"Someplace I've never been before."

Jess thought as she pulled out of the parking lot. "How about Captain's Crossing? Do you like seafood?"

Grace reflected on the question, "Do I like seafood? I have no idea. I know seafood is fish and sea creatures, but I can't recall eating it."

"Captain's Crossing serves the best crab. It's an experience you need," Jess told her.

The women were seated in a small booth. On the wall

next to them hung a fishing net filled with decorative seashells. Grace was impressed with the decor.

"In the future, when you have your very own place, you can decorate your bathroom with a net and shells," Jess suggested.

"I cannot imagine having my own place," Grace said, sighing.

"Someday," Jess assured. "You're on your way, now that you are legal."

Grace smiled. "I guess I am."

They ordered a seafood platter and two plates so Grace could taste a variety of items. She sunk her teeth into the soft crab meat.

"This is delicious," she proclaimed. "Where has this been all my life? Where have *I* been all my life?"

The friends laughed.

"A new experience, a new delight," Jess said, and they picked up their forks and continued eating.

The day Grace received her Social Security card with her own name on it felt like another occasion to celebrate. She decided to broil steaks for supper and fix a nice, tossed salad. As she and Jess chopped vegetables, they heard a knock at the door. Jess went to the door and opened it.

"Jeremy," she announced. "What do you have there?"

"This box was left at my door but has Grace's name on it."

Jess opened the door to allow Jeremy to enter. He placed a box, about the size of a toaster oven, on the table.

"I thought you might be looking for this," Jeremy said to Grace.

"What is it?" Jess asked.

Grace used a kitchen knife to open the cardboard box. "My books," she exclaimed. "I ordered these books to help me study for the test." One by one, she removed the books from the box.

"What test are you taking?" Jeremy asked.

"Grace is studying for her GED," Jess answered.

"That's great," he responded. "I admire your determination. I guess I'm surprised you don't already have your diploma. You seem like a bright person to me."

Grace gave the first response that popped into her mind: "It was a complicated time in my life."

She placed each book on the table. *Algebra for Morons, Science Made Easy, World History for Morons.*

"*Algebra for Morons*?" Jeremy asked. "That's a terrible title."

"I have to start somewhere," Grace said.

"And those questions on the test are difficult," Jess said. "You should hear them."

Jess picked up the study book. "Listen to this." She read a question from the Social Studies section of the book. It was a lengthy question that included a graphic. Jeremy leaned over to study the question.

"That would be 'Capitalism versus Communism,'" he said.

"That was fast," Jess exclaimed and checked the answer key in the back. "He's right."

"Very impressive," Grace said.

"Not really," Jess said. "Jeremy is a Social Studies teacher."

Jeremy shrugged in mock modesty.

"Listen," he said. "I'd be glad to help you study. It helps to know how to prioritize all the information in the books."

"That would be great," Grace accepted. "Thank you."

Jess added an extra plate for supper and invited Jeremy to stay.

~

Grace collected the documents verifying her name and birth date, her Social Security card, and her proof of address. She felt nervous as Jess drove her to the Department of Motor Vehicles to take her driver's license test.

"Don't be nervous. You are a great driver," Jess told her.

They arrived to find a room crowded with people. Grace took a number and sat down.

"This may take a while. It always takes a while," Jess sighed. "But it's a good place to observe people."

Grace looked at all the people gathered. Some were well-dressed and looked professional. Others appeared sloppy or dirty, giving off an uneducated appearance. *Who am I to judge others?* she asked herself. *As Grace Shepard, I don't even have a high school diploma.* It occurred to her that in her life before the accident, she could have been poor, unemployed, or dependent on help.

When her number was finally called, Grace was given a written test. Some of the answers came easily, but others required careful thought and logical thinking. She handed the test in and received a passing score.

Next came the driving test. A driving instructor slid into the passenger side of the car. Jess had reminded her to be sure to buckle her seat belt. Slowly Grace pulled away from the curb. Her evaluation was impressive.

A vision test, and photograph later, Grace was handed her temporary driver's license.

"Another hurdle cleared," Jess proclaimed.

"I can drive now," Grace said. She smiled all the way out to Jess's car. As they left the lot, Grace said, "I hate that photo of me."

Jess laughed. "Hating your driver's license photo is normal. You are normal, Grace."

Jeremy welcomed Grace into his apartment for their first study session. The floor plan was identical to Jess's place, but the decor was quite different. An ancient world map adorned the wall behind a couch. The bookshelf displayed a twelve-volume set of *The Lives of US Presidents* and an assortment of other nonfiction resources. In the corner of the room was a spinet piano.

"You have a piano," Grace exclaimed.

"It belonged to my grandmother," he said. "Would you like some iced tea before we begin?"

"I would," she said.

"Sweet or unsweet?"

"Which do you prefer?" she asked.

"I like unsweet myself, but I have sugar if you want it."

"Unsweet is fine," she smiled.

Grace set her book out on the coffee table. Jeremy brought the tea over and sat in the chair across from her.

"If we could review some of the history facts first, then move onto math," she said.

"History's my specialty," he said, grinning.

"Yes, I can see that." Grace pointed to his collection of books on the shelf.

"I like to learn," he commented. "What can I say?"

They reviewed American government. As they discussed the Founding Fathers, Jeremy brought a book over and sat on the couch next to Grace.

"Here's a picture of the Founding Fathers. As you can see, they were not all strong and handsome types."

Grace laughed. "I think Benjamin Franklin would be fun to visit with."

"Benjamin Franklin was a character. Very insightful, but quite a character."

Grace felt aware of Jeremy's closeness. "Do you play?" Grace changed the subject, catching Jeremy off guard. "The piano," she clarified.

Jeremy took his place at the piano bench. He opened the book in front of him and began to play a lively tune.

"What a fun song," she said.

After he rose from the bench, Grace took his place. Effortlessly she performed a complicated classical piece.

"That is magnificent," he exclaimed.

"Thank you. I guess we should get back to work, though."

"Music is a stimulant for brain development," Jeremy said. "I use it at school whenever I can. You'd be surprised how quiet classical music can encourage study habits."

They picked up what was left of their iced tea.

"To music," Jeremy said.

"To GED," Grace said, and they clinked glasses together.

The city bus was becoming a familiar space for Grace. On the bus, she could study people and their mannerisms. She took note of different sections of the city. Her bus ride to the Adult Learning Center held its own preoccupations. Would she pass her GED test? Would she remember all that she had worked so hard to learn these past months? Her stomach churned with anxiety.

The test was administered in a large room. Student desks were spread far apart. Grace chose a desk, checked that her pencils were all properly sharp, and took in some slow, deep breaths. When the timer began, she turned over her test booklet and started in.

It was a grueling task. Her brain felt overloaded. Several times, she put down her pencil and walked the hallway to stretch her legs. As she handed in her completed test booklet, Grace wondered if it had been a waste of time. Had she remembered what she studied? Results were promised later in the day via email.

After a short nap, Grace began to pace the floor of the apartment. When would she have the results?

"How did it go?" Jess asked as soon as she returned from work. "Have you heard anything?"

"No," Grace replied, "and it's driving me nuts. I don't know if I can take waiting much longer."

Every fifteen minutes, she checked the email on Jess's computer.

"Sit down," Jess told her. "Whatever happens, happens. You either passed, or you keep studying."

They fixed a light supper, ate, and wiped down the kitchen. After Jess swept under the table, she glanced at the computer screen and saw an email addressed to Grace.

"Grace, I think it's here."

Grace gasped. "It is," she said, almost too nervous to open it.

Grace read the email silently.

"Well?"

A smile spread across her face. "I passed. I passed the GED test."

Jess threw her arms around Grace in a congratulatory hug.

"Let's go tell Jeremy," Grace suggested. "He'll be so proud."

Deidra Wentworth

"I do not want a party," Deidra insisted.

"But you always like to party," Vance replied.

"People will express their condolences, and I am so weary of that. Besides, I am tired, Vance. I just want to be safe at home." She glared at him. "No party."

~

The stack of work on Deidra's desk offered a pleasant distraction from her fears. Deeply focused on the latest manuscript, she jumped when the receptionist announced a visitor.

Deidra gulped. *Surely my stalker would not show up here.* She pressed the intercom button. "Who is it?"

"A Mr. Holland," the voice responded.

Deidra welcomed the private investigator into her office and shut the door.

"I thought we were going to meet after work," she said.

"I decided it would be safer to meet here than either your home or my office. This is where anyone would expect you to be." He took a seat next to her desk.

"I told you about my slashed tires," she said. "That's a crime. Shouldn't it be reported to the police?"

Holland sat back in his chair. "It is a crime, but I don't think the police can do much about it at this point."

"What has to happen before they can step in? A murder?" Deidra asked. "Please go with me to the police station. They might listen to you before they listen to me."

Reluctantly, Holland agreed and pulled his car to the entrance of the publishing company. Deidra slid into the passenger seat.

"I know one of the detectives at the precinct office. His name is Foley. I've worked with him several times."

Detective Foley listened politely as Deidra told her story, taking some notes along the way.

"Do we know that the tire slashing had anything to do with your threatening messages?" he asked.

"Who else would it be?" she responded. "It makes sense."

"I understand your concern," Foley replied. "We could check the tires to determine what kind of knife was used ..."

"The tires are gone," Deidra interrupted. "I've replaced them."

Foley sighed and looked at Holland. "Have you been able to trace the messages?"

Holland shook his head. "They all come from a prepaid wireless phone."

"Ms. Wentworth," Foley said. "Until you have a suspect, there is nothing we can do. I could send someone over to patrol your area several times a day, if that would help reassure you."

Foley and Holland shook hands. "If you uncover a suspect or he asks you to meet somewhere," the detective said, "contact us."

The meeting did not go as Deidra had hoped. It was a total waste of time in her mind. Returning to work kept her busy until Arthur Wexler poked his head in.

"Who was your visitor?" he asked.

Deidra, still perturbed, answered shortly, "No one."

"Deidra, are you okay?"

"I'm fine." She managed a quick smile.

"I just want to make sure you are safe. I know the tire incident really shook you up," he said.

"Thank you, Arthur, for caring, but I really am okay."

Brynn followed Deidra home, as had been arranged. As Deidra pulled into the drive, Brynn followed her, stopping in the driveway beside the garage.

"Is there something you need?" Deidra asked.

"I think I left something here on my last visit. Could I run in and have a look?"

"Certainly," Deidra said as she opened the door and walked down the hall toward the stairway.

"Surprise!"

Deidra jumped with a start. There in the game room stood a crowd of twelve people. India was among them, and Vance stood at the doorway, a huge grin on his face.

"Welcome home," Brynn said. "I knew I left something here." She laughed.

"You refused to arrange a party, so we arranged one for you," Vance announced. He grabbed her around her waist and drew her near.

"Vance," she spoke lowly. "All I want is a drink and bed."

"Sounds good to me," he said, too loudly for her comfort.

"She wants a drink," someone shouted, and Brynn at once pointed out the table filled with alcohol choices. "Does tequila sound good?"

People entertained themselves by playing pool, watching YouTube, and generally visiting. An hour and a half later, Deidra felt trapped. Having downed several tequilas, she was feeling light-headed.

"How about showing them what we did to the rooms upstairs," Brynn suggested.

"Good idea," agreed India. "Isn't this a housewarming party? Let's see the house."

Brynn led the whole crowd upstairs and down the hall to Deidra's bedroom.

"Please don't go into my room," Deidra pleaded.

"But it's beautiful," Brynn insisted. "You should be proud."

Vance staggered in, broadcasting that the room was his as well. He and two other guys plopped down on the bed.

"Enough," shouted Deidra. "Everyone out."

She dragged Vance off the bed and began to push people out of the room.

They made their way back to the stairway.

"Everyone please go," she cried.

Vance grabbed her hand at the top of the staircase. "I wanted to surprise you."

His sour breath engulfed her. Without thinking, Deidra shoved him away.

Vance toppled down the winding steps, landing in a silent heap at the bottom landing.

Deidra paced the emergency waiting room at the hospital. Brynn and India begged her to sit down.

"I'm too nervous," she told them. "I hope he's okay."

"The doctors will take good care of him," India said as she steered her friend to a chair.

"Why did he plan that party? I told him not to."

"We're sorry, Deidra," said India. "We thought you wanted the party."

"Vance said you discussed it," Brynn added.

"We discussed it, and I said no."

The doctor stepped into the waiting room and asked, "Who is next of kin?"

"That would be me," Brynn spoke. "These are my friends."

"Let's sit down." The doctor led them to a corner of the waiting room.

"Is he going to be okay?" Deidra asked, her heart pounding.

The doctor nodded. "He should be fine. His right fibula is cracked in two places. If he's lucky, no surgery will be required. He also suffered a moderate concussion. We will keep him here overnight for observations. Do you know how this happened?"

"It was an accident," Deidra responded quickly.

Deidra and Susan Toll worked hurriedly to prepare the downstairs bedroom for Vance. Fresh sheets, extra pillows, and a good dusting were in order. Susan placed a pitcher of water and tumbler next to the bed.

"I don't mind helping, but you make sure Mr.

Montgomery understands that I am not here to be his nursemaid," Susan instructed.

They heard a commotion in the back hallway and knew that Brynn had arrived with Vance.

"In here," Deidra called to them. "We have the room ready for you, Vance. Go ahead and lie down."

Vance reached into his pocket and handed Deidra a small bottle. "My pain pills. Keep them within easy reach," he said as he lowered himself to the bed.

"One every four to six hours," Brynn told them. "He had one just before leaving the hospital."

They heard the doorbell ring while Brynn helped her brother get comfortable.

"Just rest now," Deidra said as she and Brynn exited the room. She whispered to Brynn, "I hope he's not one of those whiney-baby patients."

Brynn laughed. "He's a man, Deidra."

When they turned into the kitchen, they were greeted by Blaire Montgomery.

"Mother," exclaimed Brynn. "What are you doing here?"

"I'm here to see poor Vance. Is he okay? You said he fell down the stairs?"

"He's resting now," Brynn explained. "Except for his broken leg, he's fine."

Blaire placed a large bag on the kitchen counter.

"I'm here to nurse him back to health," she said, emptying the bag. There were a couple of new t-shirts, an assortment of teas, ingredients for soup, puzzle books, and a collection of reading materials.

"You don't have to do this," Deidra said.

"Yes, I do," Blaire snapped.

Brynn picked up a few of the items and carried them to Vance's room.

"Now tell me," Blaire said. "What really happened to Vance?"

Deidra's mouth dropped open. "He fell down the stairs. We told you that."

"But how did he fall down the stairs?" Her glare was piercing.

"There was a group of people gathered at the top step, and Vance fell," she said.

The older woman shook her head in disbelief. "Were you there?"

"Of course, it's my house."

"That's a fact I won't forget."

"Mrs. Montgomery," Deidra said. "We appreciate what you brought over for Vance, but he's in good hands. I can care for him."

"I've seen how you take care of people," she retorted. "You kidnapped my daughter to Europe and manipulated my son to move in with you."

Deidra stood speechless.

"I'm here, Vance," Blaire shouted on her way to his room. "Whatever you need, I'm at your beck and call, honey."

Grace Shepard

Jess Flynn stretched out on the couch, newspaper in hand. As Grace put away the last of the supper dishes, Jess read the want ads out loud.

"A certified nursing assistant is wanted at New Hope Care Center."

"I've spent too much time in care centers," Grace replied.

"Paraeducators are needed at a grade school. How does that sound?"

"What's a paraeducator?" Grace sat down in the recliner.

"I think it's like a teacher's helper."

"Keep reading."

"They need a delivery truck driver, a music store clerk, an accountant. How about pizza delivery? Someone's looking for a housekeeper."

"I guess I could clean houses. I've practiced enough around here."

"And you've gotten quite good at it," Jess smiled.

"Here's the number to call." She circled the ad for Grace. The paraeducator is an online application."

"I guess I could give it a try."

"How about the music store clerk?" Jess asked.

"That might be okay," Grace uttered half-heartedly.

"It requires an in-person interview. The store is downtown, near the river," Jess pointed out. "It would be on the bus route."

That night, Jess helped Grace fill out the online paraeducator application. She called the housekeeper number, but no one answered. Jess jotted down the address for the music store. Thirty minutes later, Jess printed off a letter of recommendation for Grace to carry to an interview.

"I'm thinking that by the end of the week, you will be employed," Jess encouraged.

The next morning, Grace dressed in her best pair of jeans and a loose-fitting rayon top with pink polka dots. She looked at herself in the mirror. Her brown hair, now parted in the middle, hung almost to her shoulders. Her grey eyes were neatly framed by a pair of rectangular glasses. She applied a fine layer of foundation to soften the scar and a touch of mascara.

The city bus stopped half a block from Allegro Music Store. The building, a modern structure, featured arches that framed large, tinted windows. Grace took a deep breath, pushed her shoulders back, and marched through the entrance. She was greeted by a young woman who smiled pleasantly.

"May I help you find something?"

"I'm here to inquire about the job opening," Grace said.

"Oh. Then you need to see Mrs. Price. Wait here, please." The woman scurried off to a back room.

The store felt like a music haven to Grace. Displayed

were nearly every instrument she could think of. Pianos dotted the floor, from compact to grands. Their wood shone with luster. She sat down at a baby grand and played a quick scale. One corner of the store offered musical gifts: t-shirts, scarves, hats, and toys, all expressing the enjoyment of music. Sheet music and instructional books lined the wall.

"Are you inquiring about the job opening?"

Grace turned to find a rather classy-looking woman in her fifties standing beside her.

"I'm Janet Price," the woman said. "And you are …?"

"Grace Shepard. I'm Grace Shepard."

"As you can see, Grace, we carry a large line of musical inventory. Are you a musician?"

"I play some piano," Grace said.

Janet nodded. "Maybe we can inspire you to play more piano."

She gave Grace a tour of the store and then ushered her into her office for a brief interview. Grace handed her the letter of recommendation Jess had written the night before.

"What we need is someone to help clean. Dusting, polishing, sweeping, that sort of thing. You would also need to help organize and display our merchandise. Is that something you're interested in?"

"Of course," Grace said more enthusiastically than she intended. "May I ask, where is that music coming from? I have heard music since we stepped into this room."

Janet laughed. "It's coming from our practice rooms. We have several along this hallway. We offer music lessons and rent practice rooms to students. The most important thing is to encourage customers in their musical pursuits and always greet them with a friendly smile."

~

"I got a job," Grace shouted as she entered the apartment.

Jess joined her, jumping with excitement. "At the music store?"

"Yes," Grace replied, laughing. "You should see it. It's huge."

There was a knock on the open door. Jeremy peeked in. "Do I hear celebration?"

"Grace got a job," Jess shared.

"Great! What kind of job did you get?"

"I start work at Allegro Music Store on Monday," Grace told him, glad to have another person to tell.

Jeremy's eyes widened with surprise. "Allegro? That's my favorite store. It's a music paradise."

"You've been there?" Jess asked.

"I'd live there if I could," he joked.

On Saturday morning, Jess and Grace went shopping.

"You will need a work wardrobe," Jess said. "It doesn't have to be expensive, just not jeans and t-shirts. So, where first?"

"Let's go to Walmart," Grace suggested.

She left Walmart with two pairs of slacks and three tops. Next, they went to Goodwill. Grace had fun sorting through the racks of clothing. She chose two cardigans and two skirts. Their final stop was JC Penney. Grace found some attractive but comfortable shoes, a jacket and pants outfit, and another pair of slacks.

Grace loved working at Allegro Music Store from her first day. Mrs. Janet Price, the owner of the store, supported her completely, as did Missy, who had greeted her on interview day, and several other employees.

One day, after just a couple weeks on the job, Grace was shelving new items when she felt drawn toward the grand piano in the center of the store. Taking her place on the padded bench, she played a series of classical pieces. No sheet music was needed. Upon completion, she heard a wave of applause. Everyone in the store, employees and customers, had stopped to listen.

"Thank you. That made my day," one customer said.

"Where do you perform?" someone asked.

Janet approached Grace with tears in her eyes. "My dear, how marvelous. How did you learn to play like that?"

"My mother taught me," Grace answered, having rehearsed a quick reply.

"Do you play any other instruments?" Janet asked.

Grace looked around the store. She felt no attraction to the guitars or the drums. Spying the woodwinds, she picked up a flute. With little hesitation, she put the instrument to her lips, and a sweet melody filled the store.

Again, she was greeted with applause.

"We need to talk," Janet whispered.

Within the next month, Grace began selling merchandise and giving piano and flute lessons. She spent as much time in the practice rooms as she did on the sales floor.

"You should try out for the city symphony orchestra," Janet told her. "I know your audition would blow them away. The director comes in the store often."

"Don't I need a music degree?" Grace asked.

"Orchestra members usually do have a degree, but in the end, it is the quality of their musical skills that matters."

~

Four months into her employment, Grace, tired of riding the city bus, decided she was ready to buy a car.

"But I have no credit," she told Jess. "How can I buy a car with no credit?"

"When Jarod bought his first car, I cosigned for him," Jess said. "I could do that for you as well. After all, I think of you as my younger sister."

"You would do that?" Grace asked.

"Most definitely. Find something you like, and I'll be glad to help you purchase it."

The following weekend, Jeremy volunteered to take Grace car shopping.

"It'll be as much fun for me as for Grace," he confessed. "And a lot less expensive for me as well."

Jeremy knew where all the car dealerships were located.

"Do you want a new car or a used one?" he asked as he drove through the streets of Wichita.

"I want one that runs and that I can afford," she said.

Jeremy laughed his easy laugh. "Those are excellent requirements."

Their first stop was at a large dealership. Flags waved over the parking lot. Jeremy and Grace drove slowly around to check out the inventory. Grace spotted a car that appealed to her. When they checked the price, it was way out of her budget.

After a couple of high-priced dealerships, Grace felt discouraged.

"Don't worry," Jeremy said. "Somewhere in this city is a car meant for you."

"Do you think so?" she asked.

"I do," he said. "But first I think we need something to eat. What do you want?"

Before she could respond, Jeremy noticed her staring at a Braum's Ice Cream store. Without saying a word, he pulled into the parking lot.

"How did you know what I was thinking?" Grace was amazed.

He laughed. "I guess I picked up on some vibes or something."

They both ordered double-dip specialty sundaes and sat down at a booth.

"Have you always liked ice cream?" Jeremy asked.

"As long as I can remember," Grace said, knowing he would not understand her joke.

"You said you were homeschooled?" he asked.

"Yes. My mother was a certified teacher and taught me herself. She taught everything from math to music."

"Your mother must have been an incredible woman."

Grace nodded. "She was."

"And your father?" he asked.

"My father was a dentist. He retired just before the accident." Grace felt a twinge of guilt sharing her made-up life story until she realized that as Grace Shepard, this was her truth.

"And you?" she asked. "Tell me about yourself."

"I'm not that interesting," Jeremy shrugged. "I grew up in Derby."

"Derby?"

Jeremy gave her a strange look. "Derby," he repeated. "Just south of Wichita."

"Oh, Derby," she said as if it finally clicked. "I thought you said Kirby."

They both laughed. Jeremy went on to explain that he has one sister, went to college, and teaches history at a local high school.

"Have you ever considered furthering your education?" he asked.

"Possibly."

"You ought to check out Whitbury College here in Wichita. My alma mater," he grinned.

"Is it a good school?"

"Whitbury is known for its music program. The Whitbury Symphonic Orchestra travels around and even makes recordings. They are known throughout the area. Dr. Wesley Oglesbee is its director; he's outstanding."

"Do you know him well?" she asked.

"I minored in music," Jeremy confessed. "Piano performance. I could be teaching music, but I cannot stand the sound of beginning violinists. It makes my skin crawl."

"I experience the same feeling with beginning flutists." Grace laughed freely, feeling refreshed.

After their snack, Jeremy took her to a used car lot.

"I've heard good things about this place. My sister bought a car here once," he told her.

Grace grew excited as they walked around the lot. The

prices were much more reasonable. She tried a couple of them out, testing the comfort of the front seat. When the dealer came out, he let Grace and Jeremy test-drive a couple.

By the end of the week, with the help of Jeremy and Jess, Grace was the proud owner of a five-year-old Ford Fiesta, in charcoal grey with forty thousand miles on it.

Deidra Wentworth

The doorbell chimed again as Deidra finished her makeup routine. She could hear Susan Toll greet Blaire Montgomery. Mrs. Montgomery had popped in and out for two weeks since Vance had broken his leg.

"Just go away and stay away," Deidra muttered to herself. "That woman is driving me crazy."

Deidra went downstairs to find Vance's mother emptying a white paper bag.

"What did you bring him this time?" she asked.

"Hello, Deidra," the older woman said as if she were expecting a greeting. "I brought my son a banana split."

"Sounds good."

Deidra watched as Mrs. Montgomery carefully pulled the sealed container from the bag. When she wadded up the paper sack, Deidra realized there was only one treat.

Blaire noticed the disappointed expression on her face.

"Well, what were you expecting? You are capable of

getting your own." She turned and called to her son down the hallway.

Vance had mastered his crutches to the point that he was quite mobile.

Deidra watched him devour the sundae like a spoiled child.

"Mother, this is delicious." He turned to Deidra and said, "I thought you liked ice cream."

"I'm capable of getting my own," Deidra replied, excusing herself and leaving the room.

When Vance joined her a few minutes later, he asked, "What's wrong, Dee?"

"Tell me why your mother hates me," she demanded.

"My mother does not hate you." He sat down next to her on the couch.

"You've seen the way she treats me."

Just then, his cell phone rang. "Working from home can be a pain. One moment ..." He answered the phone quietly. When the brief conversation ended, he turned back to Deidra. "What were we talking about?"

"We were discussing your mother's hatred for me."

"She's just angry about you taking Brynn off to Europe after high school graduation."

"Vance, that was ten years ago. Is there no mercy? I'm hardly the same person I was back then."

"You know how Mother is. She still doesn't think I can take care of myself."

"I've noticed," Deidra murmured.

After a three-hour stay, Deidra was delighted to walk Mrs. Montgomery to the door. She had spent most of that time chatting with Susan. Deidra stepped outside to check the mailbox as Blaire dug into her handbag for her keys. Deidra pulled out a long blue envelope with no return address. She split it open and at once went pale.

"Is something wrong?" Blaire asked. "You look like you've seen a ghost. Or maybe it is good news. Did you win the lottery? Don't be so secretive."

Deidra ran back into the house. She dashed into the room where Vance was watching TV.

"Vance," she cried. "Look at this."

He took the letter from her and read "Time is up. Take the sum of $50,000 to Globe Life Park on Sunday. Further instructions will be given you then. Do not call the cops. Ignore this and you will experience horrendous consequences."

"Oh, Vance, what do I do?"

Susan passed by the room, glancing in with curiosity.

"Call Holland," Vance instructed.

Deidra and Vance went to the room he had been sleeping in and made the call. Lee Holland responded with grave concern.

"This is serious, Miss Wentworth. I cannot stress that enough. Are you able to get the money?" he asked over the speakerphone.

"I can, but couldn't we put fake money in the envelope?"

"We are dealing with loan sharks. It may be one, but it is probably more. They are often connected to a mob. You see, even though you are not the person who borrowed the money, the shark is treating you as if you were. Loan sharking is a criminal offense that often goes unreported because the recipient is also guilty of a crime. No one cheats a loan shark without dire consequences."

"So what do I do?" Deidra felt numb with fear.

"You get the money, but don't go to the bank alone. Could Mr. Montgomery accompany you?"

"I can," Vance said.

"I suggest you go in his car," Holland said.

"Then what?" Deidra asked; her voice sounded hoarse.

"On Sunday, I will take you to Globe Life Park. The Rangers will be playing."

"My parents have season tickets," Vance inserted.

"If you can secure those tickets, that will be helpful. Miss Wentworth, you will not be alone. I'll call Detective Foley to get police presence for us."

"But the note said no cops," Deidra pointed out.

"They will not be with us, but they will be watching from a distance. I can have constant communication with them."

"Will that be safe?" she asked.

"Safer than it would be without them," the investigator assured.

After they hung up, Deidra laid her head on Vance's shoulder. He wrapped his arms around her.

"Vance," she said, "will I be safe in a huge crowd of people? Everyone will be a possible threat. I don't want to go to a Rangers' game."

"Mr. Holland and I will be with you. Think of it this way, we'll get to watch a baseball game."

Deidra rolled her eyes.

"Besides," he said as he lifted her chin to look at him. "My parents' tickets are for a luxury suite. We can be by ourselves in the suite."

"We won't be sitting in the crowded stands?"

"No. We will be safe and alone."

On Saturday morning, Lee Holland pulled a rented car into the circular drive behind Deidra's house. Quietly, she and Vance slid into the car. Deidra was wearing a denim jacket with zipper pockets. Zipped in the left pocket was an envelope holding the money, causing her to feel extremely vulnerable.

"The suite will be perfect," Holland said as he drove around the Wentworth grounds and out to the street. "It will provide a safe place for you. You two stay together at all times."

"I won't leave her side," Vance promised."

"How will I know what to do?" Deidra asked.

"They will let you know. Be alert and keep me posted on anything that looks suspicious," Holland said.

Arriving at the stadium, they entered an already crowded parking lot. Deidra put on her wide-brimmed hat and sunglasses.

"Is this the closest parking space you can find?" Vance asked.

"We want to blend in with the crowd," Holland pointed out. "It will be a good workout for your crutches."

Walking toward the stadium, Deidra's heart pounded against her chest. She felt as if she were entering the lion's den. She clung to Vance's arm as they made their way through the crowd. People stood shoulder to shoulder. She felt a slight jolt as two boys shoved their way in front of them. Others rubbed past her as if she didn't exist.

"I want out of this crowd," she told Vance.

"We're almost there," he assured her.

She saw the face of a stern woman, a man with a scraggly beard, and another one wearing a mustache and sunglasses. They all looked suspicious, and they were moving in on her.

"Get me out of here," she cried to Vance.

Deidra's breathing became a series of short gasps, and her hands shook uncontrollably.

"I can't breathe," she panted. "I can't breathe."

Holland took her arm and led Deidra to an open corner.

"It's okay, Miss Wentworth. "Calm down. It's okay."

"It's not okay," Deidra said. "I've got a pocketful of money, and the person who has been watching me for months is right here. I don't even know what he looks like."

Two men dressed in sports coats walked by, flashing them a friendly smile. The gesture gave Deidra goosebumps.

"Let's get out of here," she cried.

Vance joined them in the corner. He wrapped his arm around Deidra's waist. After a moment, he asked, "Are you ready to go up to the suite?"

She nodded.

With Vance on one side and Holland on the other, they made their way to an elevator and down a wide hallway.

"This is the suite." Vance opened the door with a key card.

Deidra was ushered into a spacious room. A large glass window looked out on the playing field with a row of ten padded chairs lined up in front of it. In the center of the room was a table with chairs around it. Toward one side was a couch and two recliners, and on the other side was a fully equipped kitchen. Two large-screen TVs hung on the wall.

Vance led Deidra to one of the observation chairs and then brought her a beverage. Once the game began, Holland stepped out. "I will be observing the hallway," he told them. "As soon as you hear something, call."

Deidra spent the first few innings of the game fumbling with her phone, expecting a message, and pacing the suite.

"Maybe he changed his mind," Vance suggested. "This could be an opportunity to enjoy some time without having to worry. Mr. Holland is just outside, and there's no way anyone could crawl up and through this window."

"Do you think he might change his mind?" she asked.

"It's possible."

When her phone beeped, Deidra shrieked. Visibly shaken, she opened the message. "Any word?" The message came from Lee Holland.

Too stunned to respond, she handed her phone to Vance who texted, "No."

Deidra and Vance sat behind the observation window. He cheered for the Rangers and described each player. Deidra gradually joined in cheering. The next time her phone rang, she answered.

"Hello?"

"Holland here. I'm about to knock on your door, and I didn't want you to be alarmed."

Vance opened the door for the private investigator.

"No contact at all?" he asked.

"Not one message," she replied.

Feeling more relaxed, Deidra slipped out of her denim jacket to settle back in her chair.

"Oh, my God," she gasped.

"What is it?" Vance was at her side.

"My pocket is unzipped," she showed them. "The envelope is gone. The money is gone."

She pulled out a folded piece of paper and handed it to Holland.

He read, "At least it's a start. Until next time. Remember, 'the eyes of Texas are upon you.'"

"But when did this happen? Nobody approached me," Deidra said in a panic.

"A quick bump or slight of the hand was all it took," the detective explained. "We are dealing with a pro."

Grace Shepard

Grace carried herself with confidence up the steps of Taylor Hall. The four-story stone building appeared enormous, as though it might swallow her up. After six months of encouragement from Janet Price at the music store and Jeremy Barton, she applied to Whitbury College. Today was her audition with the music department.

Several chairs were lined up on the second floor outside of Dr. Wesley Oglesbee's office. Grace took a seat, determined not to let her nerves get the best of her. She could scarcely hear a violin on the other side of the door. Fifteen minutes later, a tall, dark-haired woman left the room, and Grace was called in.

Dr. Oglesbee, director of the Whitbury Symphonic Orchestra, was a large man, tall and solid. In his fifties, his full head of hair was sprinkled with gray, and his glasses sat low on his nose. Dr. Oglesbee's office consisted of shelves heaped high with sheet music, as was the desk in the corner. A piano occupied the center of the room.

The director introduced himself and asked Grace, "You are here to audition on piano? Is that correct?"

"Yes," said Grace. "And I brought my flute in case I could audition on it as well."

"How long have you been playing?" he asked.

Another question to throw her off. "As long as I can remember," was her pat answer. "My mother taught me how."

"Have you performed in school or community organizations?"

"I was homeschooled, so ..." Her voice faded out.

"Well," he said rather unenthusiastically, "let's see what you can do." He motioned for her to move to the piano bench. "Did you bring any music?"

"I did not. Do I need some? I've been practicing a lot."

Dr. Oglesbee smiled gently and nodded.

Grace positioned her fingers and then launched into Chopin's "Nocturne No. 2 in E-Flat Major." Dr. Oglesbee was immediately mesmerized. Upon her completion of the piece, he asked, "Do you play by ear?"

"I can read music too."

The director laughed as he thumbed through the stack of music on top of the piano. He pulled out a booklet and set it before Grace. Sitting back in his chair, he closed his eyes as Grace flawlessly played Bach's "English Suite No. 2 in A Minor."

"Was that okay?" she asked.

"Stay right there," Dr. Oglesbee said and he stepped into the hallway. Returning, he was followed by another man and a woman. He introduced them. "This is Mr. Don

Hewitt, my assistant director, and Dr. Lorna Marsh, head of the music department. I present to you, Grace Shepard. I'd like them to hear the Bach piece, if you will."

Upon finishing the piece, all three listeners stood and clapped.

"Marvelous," exclaimed Dr. Oglesbee. "Let's hear what you can do on the flute. Do you need some music for that?"

"If you want me to use music, that would be fine." Grace replied. She placed the instrument to her lips and then hesitated. "I shall play 'Fantana Andine' by Ceasar Vivanco Sanchez."

Exquisite music floated from the silver woodwind, both fanciful and haunting at the same time. Dr. Marsh wiped tears from her eyes.

Worried that she had offended the department chair, Grace asked, "Can you give me pointers for improvement?"

Her small audience laughed with delight.

"You play magnificently, Ms. Shepard. I am in awe of such talent," exclaimed Dr. Marsh.

Grace broke out into a relieved smile. "Really?"

"Welcome to Whitbury College." Dr. Oglesbee shook Grace's hand. "We will work out a scholarship in the next two weeks, but I can tell you that Whitbury is very lucky to have you aboard."

Within the week, Grace, Jess, and Jeremy shared a meal in celebration of the full-tuition scholarship Grace had been offered by Whitbury College.

Within months, Grace's life blossomed into full bloom. Putting in thirty hours at work a week, and taking a full schedule of classes, she would wake early and return home exhausted. Any free time was used for practicing piano and flute. She often found herself tiptoeing around the apartment so as not to awaken Jess.

One evening, she bounced into the apartment to find Jess and Jeremy eating ice cream sundaes.

"You're eating ice cream without me?" she exclaimed.

"We didn't know when you'd be home," Jess said.

"I'm home now," she smiled.

"Would you like the rest of my sundae?" Jeremy offered.

"That's sweet of you," Grace said. "But that's your treat, and you should enjoy it."

"Well, you're in a good mood," Jess pointed out.

"I have a surprise." Grace was giddy with excitement.

"Have you met a wonderful man?" Jess teased.

"Oh, stop," she giggled. "Like that would happen."

Out from behind her back, Grace held up a key. Jess and Jeremy looked confused.

"Apartment 114," she announced. "I will be moving into my own apartment."

"Where?" Jeremy asked.

"Downstairs. Here at Lakewood."

With that information, Jess and Jeremy congratulated her. Jess gave her a big hug, and Jeremy high-fived her.

"But I will miss you, Grace," Jess confessed.

"I won't be far. Downstairs and around the corner is all. Besides, my schedule is so mixed up right now. This way, I can play the flute and not disturb you."

"You can still come to my place to practice piano whenever you like," Jeremy offered.

"And you know I will," Grace assured him.

The few possessions Grace owned did not take long

to move. Fellow renters, however, decided that her new apartment would be the perfect place for some of their old or excess furniture. Jess gave her a table and lamp she had stored away. Jeremy offered a bookcase he had no room for and a rocking chair he never used. Mrs. Bellamy knew someone with an extra bed and even gave Grace some blankets and an afghan.

"When I first met you," Mrs. Bellamy told Grace on moving day, "I thought you were a bit dim-witted. You looked as if you could not understand a word I said." The older woman then whispered, "But you have turned into a sweet, friendly, and talented person. I'm glad to call you friend."

Grace squeezed Mrs. Bellamy's hand.

With everything in place, Grace and her moving crew were ready for the monthly social in the activity room of the complex.

"We are welcoming a new tenant," Mrs. Bellamy told them.

It had not occurred to Grace that the new tenant was herself until they stepped into the room and she saw the banner across the windows, reading "Welcome Grace!"

As guest of honor, Grace was first in line to fill her plate with delicious barbequed pulled pork. She took a seat and was soon surrounded by other residents of the complex, all congratulating her on her own apartment.

Mrs. Bellamy stood. "I know it's not tradition, but we'd like our entertainment to be from our new official resident. Grace, will you do us the honor of playing a few pieces on the piano?"

Feeling self-conscious, Grace hesitantly moved to the piano.

"I'm not sure what you would like to hear," she said quietly.

"Whatever you've been practicing," somebody yelled.

Grace entertained them with a classical piece and then moved on to some pop. People started clapping and moving to the music. As she began to play "You Can't Hurry Love," Jeremy hopped up and sang along with her. His voice was clear and easy to listen to. Grace had never thought of Jeremy as anything but a neighbor. His appearance was plain, his height average, his brown hair somewhat shaggy, and his smile a bit bashful. As they made music together, Grace recognized feelings she had never admitted before. This man was intelligent and kind, and he had a voice that made her melt.

When the song was over, Grace looked into his brown eyes and said, "Thank you."

Jeremy's eyes twinkled as he responded, "My pleasure."

In December, Whitbury College Symphonic Orchestra performed their *Christmas Gift to Wichita*. The annual concert was attended by people throughout the area. Grace, wearing her black dress, peeked around the corner to see people lined up waiting to enter the auditorium. She was astonished at how well dressed they were. Many of the men wore jackets and ties. Women arrived in cocktail dresses or stylish suits.

Once the auditorium lights dimmed, the heavy velvet stage curtains opened to reveal the orchestra. Dr. Oglesbee stood on the podium, his baton poised. A lively English carol grabbed listeners' attention. Highlighting the concert was the "Concerto for Flute and Orchestra No. 1 in G Major," featuring Grace Shepard. It was a lively, yet airy piece, after which the audience rose with applause.

Following the concert, crowds of people passed by Grace, sharing high compliments for her talent.

"Your concerto had my heart singing," one woman in an elegant green dress told her.

"Such talent. Such talent," a tall, stately-looking gentleman said.

Grace could not recall being the recipient of such compliments. As the lobby cleared, Jeremy stepped in from around the corner. Dressed in a black suit and tie instead of his usual high school polo shirt and jeans, he presented Grace with a bouquet of roses and kissed her gently on the cheek.

"Flowers are a tradition at such events," he said, grinning.

Grace's eyes grew moist as she leaned in and took his hand. Quietly, Jeremy and Grace slipped around the corner, where they shared a deep, passionate kiss.

~

"I'm so excited about you and Jeremy," Jess squealed. She and Grace sat in Panera Bread, eating soup and a sandwich.

Grace gave a half-smile.

"What's the matter, Grace? I'd thought you'd be thrilled."

"I am thrilled. Jeremy is the kindest, smartest, most caring man I could find. I think I may love him."

Jess grinned widely. "So what's the problem?"

"How can I share my life with another person when I have no idea who I really am?"

"You are Grace Katherine Shepard. You are talented and sweet and in love."

"I need to tell Jeremy about the accident and my amnesia," Grace said softly. "He deserves to know. I wish I knew more about my background." She sighed.

They sipped their soup and chewed a bite of their sandwiches.

"I have a friend at work," Jess said. "She had no idea who her grandparents even were, so she ordered a DNA kit from Heritage.com. When the results came back, she found out that she is 64 percent Native American."

Grace perked up. "That's an idea. I would at least know if I am Italian, or Irish, or a long-lost princess from an island country."

Deidra Wentworth

Deidra sat in the corner chair of the TV room, wrapped in a blanket. She was not cold; she was comfortable. She glanced out the window at two squirrels scampering across the lawn.

"Are you going to eat lunch?" Susan asked.

Deidra shrugged.

"You need some nutrition," the housekeeper scolded. "If you're not going to eat, I won't bother fixing a thing."

Deidra had not been out of her house for three weeks. Since returning from the baseball game, she hibernated inside, afraid to go anywhere. She would watch TV, read a little, and pace the floor, peering outside the windows.

After skipping lunch, Deidra crept upstairs to stretch across her unmade bed.

Thirty minutes later, Susan slipped into the room with a stack of folded laundry.

"What are you doing?" Deidra groaned.

"I brought up clean towels for your bathroom and clean sheets for the bed. That is, if you ever get out of it long enough for me to change. You really need to get up and find something to do," Susan said sharply.

Deidra rolled over. "I know I should," she moaned.

"Have you gone through your father's files yet?" Susan asked as she placed the bedding on the window seat.

Deidra stopped short. *Why is she asking me such a question? What business is it of hers?*

"There may be some things you need to know," Susan continued. "I wouldn't wait too long. Delay only postpones things. It doesn't erase them."

The housekeeper proceeded to the next room, leaving Deidra to wonder how much Susan knew about her father's affairs.

~

About three o'clock in the afternoon, Deidra was awakened by her phone.

"Hello," she groaned.

"Hey, Deidra, how are you feeling? Are you okay?"

It was the voice of Arthur Wexler.

"Hi, Arthur. I'm okay."

"Will you be returning to work?"

"As soon as some issues are resolved," she told her coworker.

"I need to fill you in on all the work gossip." His voice was cheerful. "You've gotten behind on the news."

"I suppose I have."

"I thought maybe we could meet for coffee. It would be

an outing for you, and I could get you caught up on what's happening at Alistair-Borne."

Coffee with Arthur sounded like a casual invitation that she might enjoy. A no-pressure friendship and news from work might be fun.

"I thought we could try the new coffee house across the way from Globe Life Park. I was there about three weeks ago, and it was enjoyable. Besides, it's easy to find."

Globe Life Park! The place of her mysterious encounter. She immediately thought twice about the invitation.

"Thank you for asking," Deidra said. "It's kind of you, but I'm not ready to be out and about yet."

That night, as Vance took off his walking boot in preparation for bed, Deidra sat down beside him.

"Vance, I think I'm going crazy. I can't trust anybody anymore."

"You trust me, don't you?"

"I suppose so. But everyone else is suspicious to me. I find myself thinking that Susan Toll could be in cahoots with the loan shark."

Vance laughed. "Susan? She's strange, but really, Deidra."

"Arthur Wexler is another one," she said. "Everything he says anymore sounds fishy."

"I warned you about Wexler," Vance said.

"And then there's your mother ..."

"My mother? Deidra, you really need to get out of this house," he said. "It doesn't have to be somewhere public, but I think you need time with people you trust."

"Maybe, but I'm really scared," she whispered.

"How about my family's lake house out at White Rock?"

Vance asked. "With only people we invite. We could have a catered meal and a small band. It would be fun, Dee."

"I don't know," she shook her head. "What if ...?"

"No one suspicious will be there. Not Susan Toll, and certainly not Wexler. It will only be people I have vetted thoroughly."

~

With reluctance, Deidra drove to the lake house, with India and Brynn accompanying her. She parked her Subaru BRZ in a gravel area near the lake and walked up the stone steps to the house, her Gucci canvas beach bag hanging from her shoulder; inside the bag was the handgun she found in her father's nightstand.

The Montgomerys' lake house was a large A-framed house with lengthy windows in the front. On an upper deck, a small band was setting up. The lower deck circled around two sides of the house. There, the caterer had set up a buffet and the bartender, his long portable bar.

The band played lively, nostalgic music, which sent Deidra reminiscing her college days with Brynn and India.

"This song reminds me of that club we went to with Vance's friend," said Brynn. "Remember that drummer with the long red beard?"

Deidra laughed. "And the way he stared at India? That was so funny."

"It was creepy," said India.

Brynn brought Deidra a drink, and soon the women were moving to the music.

"It's so good to see you laughing," India told Deidra.

"I've needed to laugh," she said, handing India her empty glass. "I could use a refill too, please."

As the sun began to set behind the house, Deidra turned to fill her plate from the buffet. Coming toward her, hand in hand, were Lawrence and Blaire Montgomery. Her heart began to pound. Laying her plate down, she darted to Vance's side.

"Your parents."

"What?" he asked with his mouth full.

"You told me your parents wouldn't be here."

"I never said that. They own this place."

"Vance, you know how your mother feels about me."

"Calm down, Dee. My mother does not hate you."

"She does. How do I know she hasn't contacted the loan shark?"

"Be reasonable," he hissed, grabbing her arm.

Immediately, Deidra jerked away and headed toward the dock. She paced the length of the dock until Vance joined her in his walking boot. Shadows had lengthened and disappeared. The deck light shone down on them.

"Dee, come here." He reached out for her.

"I don't trust your mother, Vance," she said.

"You don't trust anyone," he announced. "Come here. You're drunk and upset."

Their voices carried on the breeze up toward the house, even though they were hidden by trees and brush.

"If you're that worried, dye your hair a different color, get some silly glasses, and disguise yourself."

Deidra stepped in front of him. "Leave," she shouted. "Just get out of my way."

Without saying another word, Vance turned and hobbled his way back toward the house. Deidra looked out on the lake and let her tears roll down her face. She had been holding these tears in for a long time: From the death of her parents, to the threats, to the lost money, and to this unrewarding relationship with Vance. The water was somehow soothing, with the dock light reflecting on it. As she started to settle down, she heard a rustling in the trees. She turned sharply, unable to see a thing beyond the light above her.

She gripped her beach bag tightly and called out, "Who's there?"

She listened and then gave a sigh of relief. Upon relaxing, she heard a swishing sound and the noise of breaking branches. She instinctively removed the Springfield pistol from her Gucci bag, grasped the gun firmly, and flicked off the safety. Poised to shoot, Deidra listened.

Somebody was coming after her.

The crunch of crumbling dirt sounded near. The whooshing of branches paralyzed her. All she could move was her trigger finger. The shot echoed across the lake, through the trees, and to the house.

Screams rang out.

"Vance," someone yelled. "Somebody shot Vance."

"Hurry. Somebody call 911."

Deidra dropped the pistol into her beach bag and dashed to her car, just as she heard a woman scream, "He's dead!"

It was dark, and she felt light-headed as she raced down the dirt road.

This must be a dream. This must be a dream, she repeated

to herself. She followed the road into a wooded area near the lake. The images in her headlights rocked like a boat on a choppy lake. The narrow road grew blurry, and her head began to spin. The car swerved off the road and headed toward the lake. The Subaru's hood dipped into the lake water as her front tires were stopped by mud; the engine stalled.

Deidra struggled to open the car door in the deep mud. Her sandaled feet submerged as she trudged through the muck back to the road. The road was black and silent.

Her head still spinning, Deidra leaned against a tree and threw up. Headlights approached her. She leaned out to wave down the motorist. A small cargo truck pulled to a stop. A heavy-set man in his forties hollered out his window, "Where do you need to go?"

"Where are you going?" she asked.

"Oklahoma City."

"That's where I need to go," she yelled back.

She climbed into the passenger seat.

Red and blue flashing lights illuminated the lake house. Several police cars and an ambulance surrounded the area.

"My baby," wailed Blaire Montgomery. "Somebody killed my baby."

Lawrence wrapped his arms around her. India's voice rang out. "I can't find Deidra. Where's Deidra?"

Vance was pronounced dead at the scene. Police found Deidra's car partially submerged in the lake. On the front seat sat a canvas Gucci beach bag holding a pair of sunglasses, driver's license, cell phone, and the Springfield XDM pistol. The police took down her description: female, age twenty-eight, five feet seven inches tall, blonde hair, green eyes.

The phone contained one recently received voice mail: "Miss Wentworth, Lee Holland here. I have good news. Your loan sharks have been apprehended. R. J. Reinholt and Hal Buckman were your father's contacts. Their ID has led us to a much larger ring of loan sharks. You can relax now."

Deidra stretched her legs at a truck stop in Oklahoma City. The clock read 11:45 p.m. She went to the restroom and got a drink of water, then stood outside, watching people come and go. The cool wind had picked up, and she wished she had a jacket. She wanted to get as far from Dallas and the loan sharks as possible.

"Which way are you traveling?" she asked a young couple coming out of the truck stop with a bag of snacks. They both had long, stringy hair and well-worn clothing.

"We're headed to Salina, Kansas," the man said.

"I need a ride," Deidra told them. "Would it be okay?"

The man shrugged.

"Are you okay?" the woman asked Deidra.

"I'm just tired and hungry," she responded.

"Come on, then."

The couple led Deidra to a dented gold sedan and opened the back door for her. The woman reached in the sack to retrieve a bag of corn chips and handed them to

Deidra. The car smelled of cigarette smoke. She gobbled down the chips and then sat back and drifted off to sleep.

Deidra was awakened by the sound of howling wind and torrential rain pounding the vehicle.

"Where are we?" she asked sleepily.

"Just crossed into Kansas," the man said, turning up the windshield wipers to their maximum speed.

"Be careful, Ty," the woman said.

Thunder crashed, and hail pummeled the road ahead. It was impossible to see the road.

"Slow down, Ty," the woman warned.

Before he could respond to the warning, the car swerved and skidded out of control. They collided head-on into the overpass; the car rolled over several times before landing in the ditch.

Grace Shepard

By spring, Grace's talent was recognized throughout the city. Occasionally, she would be asked to perform for charitable events. In cooperation with the Psychology Department at Whitbury, Grace also worked with children in music therapy. She enjoyed her new responsibilities and felt happy and fulfilled.

On Sunday evenings, Grace would join Jess and Jeremy for supper. They rotated who prepared the meal each week. Gathered in Grace's apartment one evening, an email popped up on her laptop. It was the results of her DNA test.

Crowding around the computer, Grace opened the email. Her results showed that she had DNA from England, Wales, Sweden, and Spain.

"What an interesting combination," Jeremy said.

Jess studied the results. "Hmmm. England must be where the name Shepard came from." She gave a quick wink Grace's way.

Grace shook her head. She had not yet told Jeremy about her amnesia. When she tried to bring it up, it felt like ancient news that made no difference anymore. She was thankful to have the trauma behind her.

After Jess returned to her own apartment, Grace and Jeremy took a moonlit stroll around the complex. Hand in hand they walked, discussing anything that came to mind. They chatted about teaching, world events, and the people who lived at Lakewood. Evenings were often spent in one of their apartments. She studied while he graded papers. Theirs was a simple, comfortable relationship. When it came time to part, there was always a goodnight kiss.

∽

On May 3, Grace's anxiety was in full mode. Her first student recital was scheduled for that evening. The past six weeks, she had spent more time practicing piano and flute than she did sleeping, eating, and studying combined. As she anxiously slipped into her sparkling blue recital dress and pulled back her brown hair, there was a knock on her door.

Jeremy stood there, a wide grin on his face and a bouquet of flowers in his hands.

"I know tradition is to present flowers after the performance, but these are for good luck."

"How lovely," Grace said as she retrieved a vase. "You are so sweet." She kissed him on the cheek.

"Are you nervous?" he asked.

"I'm trying not to be, but yes, I am nervous."

"You will perform amazingly."

"I keep telling myself that recital audiences are usually notoriously small."

"Maybe a kiss will help calm those nerves?"

She grinned. "Make it quick so I can put my lipstick on."

They leaned into each other for a passionate yet gentle kiss. Just then, his cell phone rang.

"Your phone," she mumbled.

"It can wait," he responded, taking a quick breath between kisses.

Grace stepped out on the stage of the Whitbury College auditorium, surprised to see that the room was packed with people. Jeremy sat in the front row, with Jess and Janet Price behind him. Dr. Wesley Oglesbee and Dr. Lorna Marsh occupied the center seats of the auditorium. She performed a piano piece and then played the flute. As the recital concluded, it was Dr. Marsh and Jeremy who were the first to stand for the ovation.

Afterward, her friends met her in the reception lobby. Jeremy leaned in close and whispered, "You can do what I can only dream of doing."

With pressure of the recital behind her, Grace felt light-hearted and cheerful. Three days later, Jeremy offered to prepare her dinner, and this time with no Jess. When Grace arrived home, she was surprised to see a candlelit room, with quiet music playing in the background.

"This is a special night," he told her. "This is our night."

They sat down to a meal of chicken cordon bleu, garlic

butter rice, fresh salad, asparagus in lemon butter sauce, and banana cream cheesecake bars.

"Did you fix all of this yourself?" Grace was stunned.

"Mrs. Bellamy helped with recipes, but I did most of it," Jeremy admitted.

"I'll have to thank her," Grace replied.

When the meal was over, Jeremy filled two glasses of wine and led Grace to the couch. He lifted his glass to hers and toasted, "To the most beautiful lady I have ever known."

Grace added, "To the kindest, most patient, and most intelligent man on earth."

Just as they sipped their wine, a banging sounded at the door.

"Who …?"

Jeremy set down his glass to answer the door. Grace could hear a deep, authoritative voice. In burst two law enforcement officers.

"Are you Grace Shepard?" one of the officers asked.

"I am."

"Grace Shepard, you are under arrest for the murder of Vance Montgomery."

He put her in handcuffs while the second officer read her rights.

"I don't know a Vance Montgomery," she insisted. "I never heard of him."

"This must be a mistake," Jeremy pled. "Grace would never …"

"Miss Shepard will be taken to the Sedgwick County Jail."

"No! Please! I don't know what's happening," she yelled.

As they shoved her toward the door, Grace turned to Jeremy. "Get Jess. She'll know what to do."

The officers pulled into the garage at the Sedgwick County Jail. Grace recognized the big blue building that was attached to the jail. It was the courthouse where the hearing was held to change her name. Grace was led inside to a colorless area with benches and told to sit down.

Waiting felt torturous for Grace. Her mind ran wild: *What is happening? Why are they treating me like this? I just want to go home to Jeremy.*

One of the officers had her follow him through a heavy door that required a password to enter. Grace approached a desk and was instructed to give her name.

"Grace Shepard."

"Shepard?" a solemn-looking woman repeated.

"Alias Deidra Wentworth," the officer grumbled.

The woman nodded and wrote something down. "Age?"

"I'm thirty-three now," Grace said.

She instructed Grace to go stand on a blue line. There, her picture was taken on a web cam. The officer removed the handcuffs and escorted her to have her fingerprints and mug shot taken.

"Any tattoos?"

Grace shook her head.

"Piercings?"

"Only my ears."

She was instructed to remove her earrings as they snapped a picture of the piercings.

"You get one phone call. Do you know who you want to call?"

Grace stood by a wall where a row of telephones hung and dialed Jess's number.

"Jess, you've got to help me. I don't know what's going on," she cried.

"Jeremy told me. I'm not familiar with many lawyers, so I called David Edelman. I know he is in family law, but he knows many criminal attorneys."

"I'm not a criminal."

"I know you're not. Calm down. We'll get it all figured out."

The call completed; the officer led her to a holding cell. The walls were made of concrete blocks. There were several plastic-covered slabs that served as benches, and a half wall behind which was a toilet. Other women sat in the room.

Grace perched on the edge of one of the benches. A woman with bruises on her face stared at her with angry eyes. Grace turned away.

A tiny, young woman, with freckles and green hair, laughed and asked Grace, "So what'd you do?"

"Nothing," Grace replied.

The young one laughed again and said, "I didn't do nothing either."

A guard stepped in and called one of the occupants out of the room.

"She got bailed," said the other woman. "She's gone."

After two hours in the holding cell, a female correctional officer called Grace's name. The woman was short, but tough-looking with crooked teeth.

"Where are we going?" Grace asked.

"You're getting your own cell." The officer unlocked a barred door and handed her an orange jumpsuit. "Put this on."

The cell was a tiny room, also made of concrete blocks. Along one wall was a cement slab topped with a one-inch-thick plastic mat to sleep on. A tiny sink and a toilet were the only other items in the cell.

~

Early the next morning, David Edelman met with Grace in another tiny room with a table and three chairs. A security guard stood at the door.

"What is going on?" Grace asked.

Edelman cleared his throat. "Grace, I know you have no memory beyond the accident. Apparently, as whoever you were four years ago, you shot and killed a man in Dallas, Texas. They have been searching for you ever since."

Grace was shocked, pain sliced her middle. "I killed someone?"

"Your DNA and fingerprints match that of the accused."

"What was my name?"

"Deidra Wentworth. You lived in a suburb of Dallas. You were quite wealthy."

Grace could take in no more. "Stop talking," she told Edelman. "Please stop."

"You will be extradited to Texas very soon."

"But I don't know anyone in Texas," she explained.

"I have an acquaintance down there," Edelman said. "We went to law school together. He married the smartest person in our class, and together they practice criminal law."

"What are their names?"

"John and Monica Garrett. I have been in contact with them. They know your situation. Would you like to talk with them?"

"I guess so," Grace whispered. Edelman punched numbers into his phone. "Garrett, Edelman here. The client is with me." He turned to Grace. "John Garrett would like to speak to you."

Grace took the phone and listened to a brief self-introduction from John Garrett.

"Monica and I are gathering all the information we can about your case. We understand that this is a traumatic situation for you."

"Can you help me?" Grace asked.

"We'd like to try, but you need to agree to it."

"Okay," Grace uttered.

"You should know, we believe in second chances."

~

Grace sat in a metal chair on one side of a glass window, a phone receiver at her ear. On the other side sat Jess Flynn.

"They will be taking me to Texas," Grace explained. "Mr. Edelman put me in touch with some attorneys. Jess, they say I killed somebody." Tears began to roll down her cheeks.

"Oh, Grace. I wish I could hug you. I do not know what happened in Texas four years ago, but I do know who you are now. You are not a murderer."

Grace wiped her wet face. "They took away my cross," she said.

"What?"

"The wooden cross Adelle gave me when I left the

hospital. I was wearing it like usual, and they took it. They took my earrings as well."

"I am so sorry you are going through this," Jess said, sighing.

"How's Jeremy? I put him on my visitor list. Do you know when he's coming?"

Jess looked away, taking a deep breath. "He won't be coming," she said.

"Is he ill?" Grace asked.

"He's not ill," Jess explained. "He is angry. He thinks you lied to him about who you really are."

"What?"

"He's convinced that you had disguised yourself to hide from the law. He's heartbroken, Grace."

"I was completely myself with him," Grace insisted. "I was the only me I knew how to be."

"Grace, I am with you. Even when you go to Texas, I am with you. I will spend time down there when I can, and you can call me anytime. Remember that."

Grace nodded.

~

Two days later, two officers arrived from Dallas County, Texas. Officer Sharla Morris was a sturdy-built middle-aged woman with short blonde hair. Officer Miguel Garcia looked to be about Grace's age. He was short, dark, and pleasant looking. They led Grace into the back of a white Ford van. A partition separated each row of seats as well as the windows. They exited the garage and followed the interstate out of Wichita toward Dallas.

Defendant

The Dallas County Jail presented Grace with green and white striped pants and shirt. They felt like pajamas and looked dreadful. Officer Morris led Grace to a square room furnished with only a table and three chairs. The walls were covered in tiles. One wall included a long glass window which, from the inside, appeared as a mirror. Officer Morris firmly told her to sit. A tall black man wearing a tan suit entered the room, closing the door behind him.

"Deidra Wentworth?" he asked.

"Grace Shepard," she responded.

He gave her a glare. "You used to be Deidra Wentworth?"

"I don't remember being anyone but Grace Shepard."

"I'm Lieutenant Mark Abbott," he informed her. "Where have you been the past four years?"

"I've been in Wichita, Kansas."

"Doing what?"

"First, I was in a coma. Then I was in a rehab center,

learning how to manage daily tasks. After that, I lived with Jess."

"Who is Jess?"

"Jess Flynn. She's an occupational therapist at Crestway Rehab Center in Wichita. I lived with her until I could afford my own apartment."

"How do you make a living?"

"I work at Allegro Music Store and attend college."

Lieutenant Abbott slapped an eight-by-ten photograph in front of her. "Have you seen this man before?"

Grace studied the photo of a young, attractive man with auburn hair. "I don't know who this is."

"Look closely," he demanded. "You've never seen this man before?"

"No, I have not."

Officer Morris spoke up. "Honey, this is not the time to lie."

Grace was taken by surprise. "Honestly, I have no memory of this person," she insisted. "I will tell you everything I remember, but it won't go back more than four years. I was in a car accident and suffer from complete declarative amnesia."

"That sounds convenient," Abbott growled. "Do you know how many people in here claim amnesia?" Before Grace could respond, the lieutenant answered his own question: "At least 50 percent. People get in here, and poof, they don't remember anything."

Feeling attacked, Grace began to choke. "I did not kill anyone. I could never kill anyone," she said in a broken voice.

"Then why are your fingerprints on the murder

weapon? Why was your DNA at the murder scene? Why did you run, hiding under a new identity?"

After a brief silence, Grace looked at the lieutenant. "What was the murder weapon? Where was the scene of the crime?"

Abbott unfolded a newspaper and set it on the table. "Read this headline," he demanded.

Grace read, "Daughter of Sterling Wentworth Goes Missing."

"Read the whole thing," Officer Morris instructed. "We'll wait."

"Or maybe you've forgotten how to read?" said Abbott.

Grace glared at the insensitive comment and began to read the article. She read with curiosity that soon turned to horror.

"And you think I'm Deidra Wentworth? This is dreadful."

"It has been dreadful for the family of this young man," the detective elaborated. "He was shot in the back one night at their own lake house. And what did you do? You ran. You ran and hid, building yourself a new identity."

"I didn't," Grace insisted. "I did not shoot anyone. I couldn't," she squeaked, melting into tears.

Monica and John Garrett, both in their fifties, spoke in soft voices. The perfect pair, by Grace's observation. Monica sported an efficiently cut blonde hairstyle, matching John's hair color. Both were dressed in business suits. They sat with Grace at a small round table with four attached stools; the room held several such tables.

"I'm glad to meet you." Monica smiled and extended

a hand to Grace. John reached out his hand as well. "This must be a frightening experience for you."

Grace nodded quickly.

"I've spoken to David Edelman," John said, smiling. "He has great admiration for you, and I have great admiration for him."

"Everyone here thinks I murdered someone," Grace explained. "I have no memory of anything beyond four years ago. My name is Grace Shepard. I work at Allegro Music Store in Wichita and attend Whitbury College. I play piano and flute."

"We believe you," Monica said, a hand gently touching Grace's shoulder.

Those three words gave Grace a deep sense of relief.

"We'll do everything in our power to work this mess out. First, we need to review the charges and determine your plea," John said. "You have been charged with the murder of Vance Montgomery."

"Murder?" Grace asked.

John nodded. "Premeditated."

"And if they find me guilty? What's the sentence for murder?"

Monica spoke up. "The sentence is usually life in prison—"

"Or worse," John interrupted, completing her sentence.

"Execution?" Grace whispered.

"Hopefully, we can bargain for a lesser charge. The thing is, with complete declarative amnesia, we may be able to prove incompetency to stand trial. If you have no memory of the crime, how can you help to defend yourself?"

"Is that possible?" Grace asked.

"It's a possibility," John confirmed. "There is no

guarantee, however, that the judge will agree. Murder is a serious crime."

"Even though you have no memory of the situation or the crime," Monica explained. "Your fingerprints were on the weapon, there are witnesses to your presence at the scene, and your DNA matches that of Deidra Wentworth. In other words, we know that Deidra Wentworth shot and killed Vance Montgomery. We know that in the past, you were Deidra Wentworth. We do not know the reasons, the intent, or the emotions that led to the crime."

"So what do I do?" Grace felt helpless.

"You plead not guilty," said John. "Make us a list of everyone you know in Wichita, friends, teachers, work colleagues, doctors ... And we'll go from there."

Grace's footsteps echoed through the glossy halls of the county courthouse. Her arraignment had been scheduled for 10:30 a.m., but her name was not called until 2:45 p.m. Monica and John Garrett accompanied her into the courtroom to stand before the judge.

"State your name," the judge demanded.

"Grace Shepard."

The judge studied the information before him. "Grace Shepard, aka Deidra Wentworth?"

"Correct," Grace said, still not quite believing she was ever known as Deidra Wentworth.

"You are being charged with the murder of Vance Montgomery. Will you need the court to appoint a lawyer?"

"No, your honor," Grace said. "The Garretts will be representing me."

"I see," the judge said, nodding. "And how do you plead?"

With as much power behind her voice as she could collect, Grace said, "Not guilty."

Monica Garrett gave Grace a slight nod of approval.

"As far as bail is concerned," the judge continued, "between the severity of the crime and the fact that you vanished for four years, I must consider you a high flight risk. You will remain in custody until the time of your trial. Next case."

Defendant

"That's her." Grace could hear them whisper as she was handed a cheese sandwich and sliced fruit for lunch.

Somebody shouted, "Hey, that's the Runaway Rich Girl."

Grace tried to ignore them. She longed to fold up into a shell and hide from the world.

Splat! Spittle landed on her arm.

"Did you think you could get away with murder just because you're rich?"

As the women dispersed, a skinny inmate with long, straight hair slapped a newspaper next to Grace. "It don't look like you," she said. "But we all know it is."

Grace glanced down at a front-page article. "Deidra Wentworth Arrested for the Murder of Vance Montgomery." She read on: "Tagged as the Runaway Rich Girl, the daughter of Sterling Wentworth of Dehlco Petroleum Corporation has been discovered in Kansas. Living under the assumed name, Grace Shepard, her identity was revealed through a DNA match."

Grace examined the photograph of an attractive woman with long, wavy blonde hair and glistening green eyes. She looked like a beauty queen.

That is not me, she thought. After all, Grace's hair was brown, and her eyes were grey, under her very necessary pair of glasses. There was no scar on the face of Deidra Wentworth. She stared intensely. There may be something familiar about the curvature of the mouth, and perhaps the shape of the eyes. *Is it possible?* She began to wonder.

Later that afternoon, a security guard approached Grace. "I need you to come with me," she said.

"Do I have a visitor?" Grace was hoping.

The guard led her through a set of heavy doors and down a lengthy hallway. She stopped in front of a barred door. On one side was a plexiglass window that looked in on a small cell. "Where are you taking me?" Grace asked as the guard unlocked the door.

On either side of the cell were two small built-in steel cots with one-inch plastic foam pads. There was a small sink and a toilet. On one of the cots sat a weary-looking woman in her forties. She had deep creases in her face, and gray hair accented her temples. She stared at Grace through sympathetic brown eyes.

"This area is for high-profile cases," explained the guard. "Nobody cares who you are here."

The walls were made of cinder blocks, giving the tiny room a cold appearance.

"This is Rhonda," the guard said.

The older woman nodded.

Rhonda turned out to be friendlier than Grace had expected.

"What are you in for?" she asked.

With some hesitation, Grace said, "They think I murdered a man four years ago."

After a pause, Rhonda asked, "Did you?"

"I don't know," Grace said.

"Why? Were you drunk?" Rhonda was direct.

"I was in a wreck soon after the event. I spent weeks in a coma and remember nothing. The doctors say, I may never remember."

Rhonda thought about what Grace had told her. "So you really don't know if you killed somebody."

Grace nodded. "How about you? What are you in for?"

In a matter-of-fact voice, Rhonda said, "Murder."

"Were you drunk?" Grace asked.

Rhonda broke into a slight smile. "I was not drunk. I killed my son."

Grace could not imagine killing one's child.

"He was twenty-three, had schizophrenia. From the time he was five years old, I had him in counseling. People just thought I was a bad parent. Do you have any kids?"

Grace shook her head. "What was your son's name?"

"James. His name was James, after his dad."

"Is his dad still around?" Grace asked.

"Nah," said Rhonda. "He left when James was nine. He couldn't take it any longer." Rhonda stretched out on the cot and stared at the ceiling. "James destroyed his dad's car, pulled doors off their hinges, killed his pet rabbit, and since he was thirteen, he threatened me on a regular basis."

Grace tried to comprehend this kind of behavior.

"The car was the last straw for him. I can't really blame him."

"So, you raised James alone after that?" Grace asked.

"I tried. James was in and out of detention centers from the time he was ten. Spent time in psych hospitals, but only for a few days here and there. Staff thought he was a sweet little boy."

"What finally happened?"

"James hallucinated. He saw people living in our attic and thought they wanted to hurt us. One day, I went out to the shed where James was working. He had a look of horror on his face. Thought I was one of the dangerous people. Came at me with a shovel." Rhonda sat upright. "I grabbed a mallet, and with all my might, I swung it at him. Hit him in the head. He fell down dead."

Grace wiped tears from her eyes. "I'm sorry."

"It's not your fault I'll get the needle."

"The needle?"

"Lethal injection," Rhonda clarified.

"Do you have a lawyer?"

"Of course, but will a jury believe it was self-defense? Especially since I buried James on the farm. The neighbor's dog found him. So I was arrested for his murder, and the governor has promised to be tough on crime. I know I'll get the needle."

"But you had every reason to fear your son, every reason to defend yourself," Grace argued.

"Tough on crime," is all Rhonda said.

Grace sat with Monica and John Garrett at a small consultation table, while in the background, they could hear inmates arguing. Monica greeted her with a wide smile.

"You have some amazing friends," she said. Monica pulled a file from her briefcase. "First, I talked to Dr. Dean Milton."

Grace felt a sense of relief at the mention of his name.

"He sent us his medical evaluations of you and information on the diagnosis of complete declarative amnesia," she reported. "Apparently, the fact that you are alive is nothing short of a miracle."

"What does that have to do with whether Deidra Wentworth shot that guy?"

"It provides medical proof that you have no memory of the incident nor the circumstances that led up to the crime," John spoke up. "The doctor stressed that the memory is lost forever. You will never remember the life you had before the accident."

Monica flipped to another page. "I also talked to Dr. Ted Yates."

Grace could not help but smile. "Dr. Ted is so kind," she said.

"He's a highly respected psychiatrist," John added.

"What did he tell you?"

"He assured us that you have been through a tremendous trauma, both physically and emotionally. He admires your progress and has reason to believe you are on your way to a productive and successful life," Monica explained.

"I wish I could talk to him now," Grace admitted. "Did you contact anyone else?"

"Jessica Flynn?" Monica spoke in a question.

"Jess!" Grace stood with excitement. "You spoke to Jess?"

"I can only say that I wish I had a friend as loyal as Jess is to you," Monica said.

"I miss Jess so much," Grace murmured.

Monica pulled a folded paper out of the file and handed it to Grace. "Jess wasn't sure of the address. She emailed a letter to us so we could deliver it."

With the passion of a starving animal, Grace delved into the letter:

> My dear Grace, I have not slept well since they whisked you away. Hoping you are safe. I feel better having talked to the Garretts. They, like I, know that you are innocent. I miss our talks and all the laughter. If it is any consolation, I imagine I am with you every evening as I eat supper. Jeremy is still confused. He feels as though he was misled. I will continue to explain that you presented to him the only person you know how to be.
>
> I will love you forever, like a little sister, and will write again very soon.
>
> Always,
> Jess

Grace allowed tears to roll freely down her cheeks. "Do you think you can convince the court that I am innocent?"

John spoke softly. "The first thing we will do is ask for a competency hearing. That will mean undergoing a psychological evaluation."

"You want people to think I'm crazy?" Grace asked.

"No, of course not," Monica said quickly.

"If we can prove that you have no memory of life as Deidra Wentworth, how can you possibly speak in your own defense during trial?" John explained. "That would violate your constitutional right to a fair representation."

"And," Monica added, patting the folder in front of her. "We have professional testimonies that address the issue."

~

Dr. Joseph Scully was a short, stocky, bald man. His glasses were too large for his round face. He met Grace in a conference room, furnished with nicely padded chairs and a large table. A small kitchen at one end of the room was supplied with beverages and snacks. Dr. Scully, a forensic psychiatrist, had been sent over from the Texas State Mental Hospital.

He began his assessment by placing a test booklet in front of Grace. The doctor sat in a corner chair, reading his iPad, while Grace answered pages of strange and intrusive questions: "I think somebody is following me. I have a good appetite. I have diarrhea once a month or more." Such questions continued for pages. By the time she finished, Grace felt blurry-eyed and weary.

"Time for a snack," announced Dr. Scully. From the kitchen, he brought out some sandwiches and potato salad, and then he asked Grace what she wanted to drink. He threw out some general questions about her, gradually moving toward the case.

"What do you remember about the death of Vance Montgomery?"

"Nothing," she said. "I haven't any idea who Vance Montgomery was."

"What do you know about him?"

"Only that he was wealthy, and that Deidra Wentworth shot him. Wasn't it at a lake?" she asked.

"Do you know what Vance looked like?"

"I've only seen one photo of him. He appeared neatly groomed."

"What do you know about the charges against you?" Dr. Scully asked.

"I'm charged with murder. Police think it was planned and intentional. It means that Deidra Wentworth set out to kill Vance Montgomery that day."

"That's right," he said. "Who is your attorney?"

"I have two attorneys," Grace told him. "John and Monica Garrett."

"And what's the job of an attorney?"

"Their job is to defend me. They need to convince the jury that I am not guilty of the crime."

"What is the job of the prosecution?"

"The prosecution has the burden of proving that I am guilty of the crime."

Questions continued, often repeated or said in a different way. After five hours in the conference room, the psychological evaluation ended. Grace was led back to her cell, where all she could do was await the results.

Defendant

The large courtroom was almost empty. Grace, wearing her green and white stripes, sat before the judge, between Monica Garrett and John Garrett. Across the aisle, Loma Calero, the district attorney, stood in a professional three-piece suit. The DA exuded professionalism. She appeared poised and confident.

So that is the woman who will try to prove my guilt, Grace thought.

"How would you assess Ms. Wentworth's intelligence?" she asked Dr. Scully, who occupied the witness stand.

"She is obviously an intelligent person," the doctor responded.

"Would she have the ability to understand legal proceedings?"

"She has a clear understanding of legal proceedings and articulates it well."

The district attorney moved toward her seat before

turning abruptly. "Dr. Scully, I'm curious, how often is amnesia claimed in murder cases?"

"Objection!" Garrett shouted. "I am not aware that this witness is an expert in statistics."

"Objection sustained," the judge decreed.

"Would you say that amnesia is easy to fake?" Calero asked.

"Some forms of amnesia are quite easy to fake. An amnesia claim can also be difficult to prove."

"In summary, then, you believe that the defendant is capable of working with her attorney and understanding directions?"

"Absolutely."

"No more questions." Calero took her seat.

John Garrett approached the witness stand, rubbing his chin in thought. "Dr. Scully, you mentioned that there are several types of amnesia. Give us some examples."

"Anterograde amnesia results from brain trauma. The patient is unable to recollect events after onset for more than a few minutes. Day-to-day functional memory is poor. Retrograde is another form of amnesia in which the patient is unable to recall events before amnesia set in. The early memory is safe, with memory decline building up to the event."

"You're saying that childhood memories would be intact?" Garrett asked.

"Yes. Childhood memory would be there; however, events leading up to the brain trauma would not. With dissociative amnesia, the patient cannot remember personal information. This might be experienced by someone who witnessed a violent crime. There is no identity crisis, but they move through a trancelike state and develop depersonalization to block out stressful experiences."

"Would you say that the defendant suffers from any of those forms?"

"I would not," Scully answered. "Her day-to-day memory is intact, ruling out anterograde. Ms. Wentworth appears to have lost all memory of her early life, which does not happen with retrograde. Her identity crisis would rule out dissociative amnesia.

"Have you heard of complete declarative amnesia?" John asked.

"Declarative amnesia is rare," explained Scully. "Complete declarative amnesia would be exceptionally rare. I have not encountered it in my practice."

"But it is a real condition?"

"It is real. If the temporal lobe is damaged to a life-threatening extent, a patient would lose all recall of past experiences. Recall of learned information might remain, but an intense identity crisis would certainly ensue."

"Is there any chance that a patient with complete declarative amnesia would, at some point, undergo a restoration of their past experiences or identity?"

"Like I said, I have not encountered this phenomenon in my years of practice, but by the mere severity of the brain damage, I would say, no."

Judge Sloane explained that he would review the competency evaluation and send his determination promptly to both the prosecution and the defense.

Grace returned to an empty cell. Rhonda's trial had begun. She wondered what was happening in the courtroom. Would they show any compassion to her cellmate? While at her lunch table, Grace noticed a new inmate in the high-profile area. She was a slight, young woman who looked more like a child than an adult. She was, however, quite pregnant.

"Did you just arrive?" Grace asked, setting her tray across from the young girl.

"Uh huh," she acknowledged. "They put me here today."

Grace noticed a slight speech impediment.

"I'm Grace. What's your name?"

The young girl chewed a bite of bologna sandwich. "Jewel," she said.

"How old are you, Jewel?"

"Twenty-four," Jewel said. Grace thought she looked more like fourteen.

"When is your baby due?"

"Doctor says pretty soon."

"Are you scared?" Grace asked out of genuine concern.

"Sometimes. I get scared about the baby popping out."

"What were you put in here for?"

With noticeable hesitation, Jewel said, "Rape."

"Somebody raped you?" Grace was confused.

Jewel shook her head. "Not this time. People say I raped somebody."

The idea seemed unthinkable to Grace. How could this tiny person rape somebody? "Who says you raped someone?"

"Juan's mama and daddy. They say I raped him, but it's a special kind of rape."

"Statutory rape?" Grace asked.

"Uh huh. They say I statutory raped Juan."

"Do you know how old Juan is?"

"Sixteen. Juan is sixteen. He's my baby's daddy." Jewel smiled as she patted her stomach.

After lunch, Grace and Jewel sat in the dayroom with books and board games. Grace felt a need to befriend this poor girl.

"Don't be afraid to talk to me," she told Jewel. "We all have problems here. Tell me about Juan."

Jewel's eyes sparkled as she spoke of Juan. "Juan and me wash dishes at the Star Diner. His mama's and daddy's diner. We love each other. Juan will talk to me. He's so nice. Other people just want to hurt me, but not Juan."

"What people want to hurt you?" Grace asked.

Jewel let out a long sigh. "I used to babysit for kids next door. Mama made me because she don't have a car, and we needed groceries. The man next door would come home and take me into the bedroom and make me do bad things. He hurt me. I begged Mama not to make me go there anymore, but she forced me to. He raped me over and over."

Grace could not control the tears that blurred her eyesight. Her heart broke for this child. "I am so sorry," she said, hugging the young girl.

Jewel leaned into the hug.

"Don't be afraid," Grace whispered, but in fact, Grace was afraid for her young friend. *How can the world be so cruel?* she wondered.

When Rhonda was brought back from court, she lay down without saying anything to Grace.

"Do you want to talk about it?"

Rhonda rolled over, facing the wall.

Grace felt weighted down. She faced her own accusations, but she realized that everyone in this place represented some sort of tragedy, some sort of desperate situation.

As day moved toward night, she could hear Rhonda's breathing float toward sleep. Grace knelt by her cot. She placed her fingers on the mattress and imagined herself at a grand piano. Her fingers glided across the keyboard, the most comforting music arising in her imagination. She felt as though someone were standing by her. She knew it was Jeremy.

A guard opened Grace's cell.

"You have a visitor," she announced. "Your attorney is here."

Grace followed the guard to the visiting room. A line of telephones hung on the wall next to a series of windows. Grace sat on a chair, with Monica Garrett on the other side of the window. She put the phone to her ear.

"Grace," said the attorney, "I brought you a visitor."

"Jess? Jeremy?" Grace exclaimed.

"No. It's not anyone on your visitor list. She insisted on seeing you, so I agreed to bring her with me."

Puzzled, Grace watched a dark-haired woman take the chair next to Monica. Covering the receiver to muffle their voices, Monica appeared to be reviewing guidelines for the visit.

"Deidra," said the woman, her brown eyes moist. "Don't you remember me? I'm India, your best friend."

Grace shook her head quickly. "I don't know you."

"Oh, Deidra, you scared me so badly. No one knew what happened to you. At first, they thought you had been kidnapped or maybe drowned. When I heard they had found you, I was so relieved." India studied the face on the opposite side of the glass. "What happened to you, Deidra? You look so different."

"I was in a bad accident. I guess I almost died. I have no memory of my life before the crash."

"Your hair," India pointed out. "You used to keep it colored blonde. You would tell me that you identified as a true blonde. And your eyes. I remember a time you refused to wear glasses in public. You purchased those gorgeous green contact lenses."

Grace listened, as if to gibberish, having no recollection of who this stranger was. Finally, she asked, "Did I kill that guy?"

Immediately, Monica Garrett flashed a look India's way and mouthed something to her.

"Deidra, you were scared. You were petrified. I miss you so much."

~

When Rhonda returned to the cell after her second day in court, she plopped down on her cot.

"Talk to me," Grace begged. "What's happening in the courtroom?"

"You know," she sighed. "I never felt like anyone understood what I went through raising James. Why would I think they might understand James's death?"

"You must cling to some hope," Grace suggested.

Rhonda rolled her eyes with annoyance. "Hope. How

can I cling to hope when all people want is to show they are tough on crime? I committed a crime."

"It was in self-defense."

"The court doesn't care."

"Would it be different if you'd given James a proper funeral?" Grace asked.

After a long pause, Rhonda said, "What nobody understands is that I buried James on the farm so I could have my troubled baby near me. He was finally at peace, and I wanted him close."

~

Grace sat at a small, round consultation table with the Garretts. John pulled a small stack of papers from a manila envelope.

"We have the results of your competency hearing," Monica began.

"What did the judge decide?" Grace asked.

John spoke, "First, it states that you were properly informed of the charges and the procedures. It lists sources of information, predominantly Dr. Scully. It includes some relevant history and the circumstances of referral."

"What did the judge decide?" Grace repeated.

John continued, "It states your ability to stand trial, and …"

Monica cleared her throat. "John, tell her what the judge decided."

John paused to regroup. "The judge concludes that evidence indicates that you have a clear understanding of the charges and the ability to participate in the proceedings. Although the likelihood of complete declarative amnesia may restrict your memory of events, to declare you incompetent to stand trial would initiate the protocol of placing you in a state-approved treatment program in a state mental hospital. In the judge's opinion, that is not what you need. Currently, you are mentally sound with a more than adequate understanding of charges and court procedure." He placed the papers back into the envelope, took a deep breath, and said, "Grace Shepard, let's prepare for trial."

Defendant

While Monica Garrett actively gathered testimonies for trial, John kept Grace informed. "I have a question to ask you," he said one afternoon. "Would you be willing to submit to a polygraph test?"

"A lie detector test?"

"That's right. It would not be admissible in court; however, it would show your willingness to cooperate. If the results come out favorable, I would consider bringing the results to the attention of the judge. Best case scenario, your case would be thrown out or the charges reduced."

"Is that a possibility?" Grace asked. "Of course. I will take a polygraph.

~

Grace clung to the thread of hope that her case might be thrown out. She felt a surge of energy when she ate supper that night. Rhonda had been found guilty of homicide and awaited her sentence. She barely ate a bite. Jewel did not feel hungry either, so Grace ate alone, praying with every bite that the polygraph would help her case.

At 12:45 a.m., Rhonda and Grace were awakened by a loud cry.

"What the hell is that?" Rhonda exclaimed.

The sound continued. "Is somebody hurt?" Grace wondered.

Footsteps sounded in the hallway. The women looked out from the barred window just in time to see a wheelchair rush past. Moments later, two guards pushed Jewel down the hall.

"She's in labor," Grace stated.

"She's just a child herself," said Rhonda.

"Twenty-four," Grace informed.

"She can't be that old. She's such a little wisp."

As the hall quieted, they returned to their cots, but Grace was unable to relax. The thought of Jewel giving birth without a friend or family member near deflated any sense of hope she may have felt earlier.

~

John Garrett requested a polygraph expert be brought to the jail to administer Grace's lie detector test.

A guard led her to an interview room, where the equipment had been set up.

"How long will this take?" Grace asked.

"Probably longer than you're hoping," the guard responded.

The polygrapher welcomed Grace and asked her to sit in

the chair in front of the table. Despite his pleasant demeanor, Grace thought the man looked like the stereotypical liar. His narrow eyes, thin mouth, and pockmarked face drew a sinister profile in her mind.

He attached two straps around her middle and a blood pressure cuff around her arm. Two of her fingers were wrapped with other wires.

"Is your name Sally?" he asked.

"No." *What a waste of a question*, Grace thought.

The first several questions had obvious answers, and she began to relax. From there, questions grew more precise, sometimes with complicated wording, so Grace had to be attentive to her responses. By the end of the procedure, Grace felt physically and mentally exhausted.

Grace waited for John Garrett to arrive with the completed report. He met her at the little round table that afternoon. The outcome stated that her physiological response to diagnostic questions gave no indication that she responded with anything but the truth.

The next day, Grace followed the guard to the visitor room. When she viewed the person on the other side of the window, Grace was overjoyed.

"Jess!" she shouted with delight. "I am so glad you're here."

"Are you okay?" Jess asked.

"I eat and sleep. I have two encouraging attorneys."

"You do," Jess agreed. "Mrs. Garrett came to Wichita to interview me. I have been called as a witness for the defense."

"Wonderful," Grace exclaimed. "But my trial hasn't started yet. Why are you here now?"

"I'm taking a family leave from my job so I can be down here with you."

"Family leave?"

"You are my little sister, remember?"

"Oh, Jess, having you here makes everything so much better," Grace said.

"How are things looking?"

Grace shook her head. "I really don't know. I don't even know if I am guilty or innocent."

"I do," said Jess. "You are innocent."

"But how do you know for sure?"

"Because you are Grace Katherine Shepard, and I have known you all your life. You are kind, talented, and honest."

"People think I should pay for a crime I committed before Grace Shepard existed. They call me the Runaway Rich Girl."

"You're rich?" Jess asked.

"Deidra Wentworth was a rich woman from Dallas. I'm a poor music student from Wichita."

"All I can tell you, Grace, is that the Garretts will do everything they can. David Edelman thinks very highly of them."

A silence followed. Grace lifted her head and asked, "Is Jeremy okay?"

"Jeremy keeps teaching and eating and flattering Mrs. Bellamy. But Grace, Jeremy needs time to work through all of this."

"Does he still think I hid the truth from him?"

"He's hurting," Jess said. "But I can tell you this: Jeremy

is in love with Grace Shepard. He just doesn't know what to do with Deidra Wentworth."

"Neither do I, Jess. What do I do with Deidra Wentworth?"

Two days after giving birth, Jewel returned to the county jail. She refused to speak or look at anyone. She sat in the corner of the day room, rocking back and forth. As others were leaving the room, Grace sat down beside her.

"I'm worried about you," she said softly. "Tell me what happened."

Jewel turned away.

"I'm not going anywhere until you talk to me," Grace told her.

There were three minutes of silence before Jewel burst into tears. "They took my baby," she wailed. "They took my baby away from me."

Grace wrapped her arms around Jewel's tiny body. She brushed her hair away from her face and whispered, "Tell me about the baby; a boy or a girl?"

"A girl," Jewel whimpered. "A girl with fuzzy brown hair."

"Did you get to hold her?"

Jewel nodded. "But when I wanted to feed her, she was gone. I never saw her no more."

"You poor child," Grace said, sighing. "Do you know where they took her?"

"No. The nurse said she was given to a family who can love her. But I … I …" Jewel stammered and then said, "I was gonna love her. She was gonna love me."

"Did you choose a name for her?"

"Uh huh. Her name is Violet. My favorite color."

Grace walked Jewel back to her cell. She led her to the cot, placed a blanket snugly around her, and gently stroked her hair until she fell asleep.

Grace listened as Monica and John Garrett prepared her for trial.

"We have a list of character witnesses," Monica assured her.

John spoke up. "This is not your ordinary murder trial. The defendant cannot speak for herself. The crime took place over four years ago. The defendant and the accused don't even share the same name." He sounded irritated.

Monica interrupted her husband's rant. "We had hoped for an incompetency ruling, but that didn't happen. We hoped the polygraph would influence the judge, but we haven't heard back about that."

"What else do we have?" Grace asked hesitantly.

"We have a defendant who is plainly not the same person as the accused," John explained. "Our contention will be that on the day of the car accident, Deidra Wentworth died. From that moment, she no longer existed. The woman who awoke from a coma had no memory, no past experiences, no record of education, no employment history, and no relationships. Deidra Wentworth died. Grace Shepard is a completely different person who has fought for everything she has accomplished."

"Will it work?"

Monica Garrett provided Grace with a professional-looking black and burgundy pantsuit. She helped brush out her hair and applied a splash of makeup to her face. As the three entered the courtroom, Grace appeared more confident than she felt.

They stood as Judge Murray Sloane entered the courtroom. Grace could not read his face but found the flowing black robe intimidating. He appeared to be in his sixties with short, gray hair and a pleasant face.

"Ladies and gentlemen of the jury," the judge began, "you have been selected as the jury in the matter of the *State of Texas versus Deidra Wentworth*. Miss Wentworth is charged with the murder of Vance Montgomery. She has entered a plea of not guilty to these charges." Judge Sloane proceeded to instruct the jury on their role and the law. "The defendant is presumed innocent until proven guilty beyond a reasonable doubt, and the burden of proof is on the state. For the past four years, the defendant has been living as Grace K. Shepard. Note that both the name Deidra Wentworth and Grace Shepard refer to the same individual."

Grace studied the jury. The woman on the end looked like someone who would be a nice neighbor. A man on the top row sported a white beard, reminding her of Santa Claus. The Hispanic boy on the front row could not be over twenty-one years old.

Loma Calero clicked across the floor in her high heels to make her opening statement.

"Four years ago, on the night of June 5, Vance Montgomery was shot and killed while attending a party at the Montgomery family lake house. He was shot with a Springfield XDM that was found in a beach bag belonging to Deidra Wentworth. The DNA matches that in Miss Wentworth's abandoned car, and her fingerprints were found on the murder weapon. We intend to prove beyond a reasonable doubt, by physical evidence and the testimony of people who know her, that Deidra Wentworth intentionally shot and killed Vance Montgomery."

When it was time for the defense to give their opening statement, John Garrett sat silent for several seconds. Slowly, he rose and made his way to the jury. He cleared his throat. "You have been selected to serve as jury for a case like no other. A person is dead, but the defendant is innocent. The victim of a deadly accident, Grace Shepard has no memory of life as Deidra Wentworth. She has no memory of the victim or the circumstances leading up to his death. I am here to prove that where there is no recall, there can be no guilt. What is being attempted by the prosecution is equivalent to punishing one generation for the crime of the previous generation. Grace Shepard is a different person from Deidra Wentworth. I implore you to listen with an open mind. Listen with a compassionate heart."

Defendant

The first witness to be called by the prosecution was Lieutenant Mark Abbott of the Dallas County Sheriff's Department.

"Tell us what happened on the night of June 5, 2016," DA Calero said.

Grace recognized the officer as the one who had questioned her upon her arrival at the county jail.

"We received a call at 9:07 on the night of June 5. Someone reported a shooting incident at White Rock Lake with one man down. Arriving at the scene, we found the victim, Vance Montgomery, with a bullet in his chest. It had entered through his back, and he was dead upon our arrival."

"Who else was at the scene of the crime?" the district attorney asked.

"There was a crowd of people, including the caterer

and a small band, along with the guests. People were screaming and crying."

"Was Deidra Wentworth present?"

"I didn't see her; however, people were looking for her, so I know she had been present."

"Did you search the area for a possible shooter?"

"Of course. What we found was an abandoned car with its front wheels stuck in the mud of the lake."

"Describe the car you found."

"It was a Subaru BRZ. A pearl white exterior. License plate number LWP 7442."

"Did you run a check on the plate?"

"Absolutely. The car was registered to Deidra Wentworth."

"Was anyone or anything in the car?"

"Nobody," the lieutenant said, "although the driver's door had been left open. Contents included a canvas Gucci beach bag containing a pair of sunglasses, a cell phone, a driver's license, and a handgun."

Calero brought forth a beach bag, holding it up for the witness to inspect. "Is this the bag you found in the car?"

Lieutenant Abbott looked over the bag carefully. "It is," he confirmed.

"Let us mark the bag as Exhibit A."

Almost immediately the district attorney presented Exhibit B, a handgun.

"Do you recognize this gun?" she asked.

"That is a Springfield XDM pistol," he explained. "The same gun found in the beach bag. The same gun that killed Vance Montgomery."

"And to whom is the gun registered?"

"It is registered to Sterling Wentworth," he said.

"Are there safety features on this handgun?"

"There are safety features," Lieutenant Abbott stated. "For one thing, it has a trigger safety and an internal firing pin safety. There is also a backstrap safety, which means you must be gripping the gun for it to fire. The indicator on the top of the gun tells you if it's cocked and ready."

"Explain to the jury how a trigger safety and internal firing pin works."

"The trigger safety releases when you have a good grip on the pistol. It rests on the grip between your thumb and trigger finger. The firing pin prevents accidental discharge if the handgun were dropped."

"How hard would it be for this type of gun to accidentally discharge?"

"Accidental discharge is extremely unlikely with a Springfield XDM."

Calero turned toward her seat. "No more questions."

John Garrett rose slowly, standing in silence for a few seconds.

"You confirmed that the Springfield DXM was indeed the weapon used to shoot Vance Montgomery. From what distance was it shot? Was it from close range or otherwise?"

"The forensic report estimates that the gun was fired from around twenty yards away."

"Twenty yards, you say. Was that twenty yards of open range or was it through trees, brush, or other objects?"

"The weapon was fired from near the dock, and the victim fell partway up the hill, between the dock and the house."

"What's in that space?"

"It's a relatively densely wooded area."

"At that time of night on June 5, was it still light or was it dark?" Garrett asked.

"The sun would have already set. So it would have been dark at the time."

"Twenty yards, through a wooded area, in the dark … That must have been a damn good marksman." Calero moved to stand up, but before she could object, Garrett added quickly, "No further questions, Your Honor."

The second witness to be called by the prosecution was Brynn Montgomery. Grace watched a stylish woman with spiky auburn hair take the stand. Her teeth were strikingly white.

Calero asked, "How do you know the victim, Vance Montgomery?"

"He was my brother," said the witness.

"And the defendant? How long have you known Deidra Wentworth?"

The witness glanced up at Grace. "Deidra and I went to high school together and have been friends ever since."

Calero held up the canvas Gucci beach bag with red and green along the top. "Have you ever seen this bag before?"

The witness nodded. "It belonged to Deidra. I was with her when she purchased it."

"When was the last time you saw it?"

"Four years ago, on June 5, the day of the lake house party. Deidra had the bag with her."

"You saw her with this bag on the night of the murder?"

"I did," Brynn said. "In fact, I rode with Deidra to the lake house and had to remove the bag from the passenger seat before I could sit down."

"Were you aware of the contents of the bag?"

"I know she dropped her sunglasses into the bag. Other than that, I didn't look inside."

"How would you describe Miss Wentworth's disposition on the night of the lake house party?"

"Objection," John Garrett interrupted. "Calls for speculation."

"Overruled," Judge Sloane replied. "Tell us your perspective, Miss Montgomery."

Brynn repositioned herself in the witness chair. "Deidra was frightened that night. She had been frightened for weeks."

"Why was she frightened?" Calero asked.

"After her father's estate was settled, Deidra started receiving threatening messages. She believed that somebody was out to harm her. The lake party was planned to help her relax."

"Did she relax that night?"

"After a few drinks, she was laughing," Brynn reported.

Calero thought for a moment before saying, "You said you rode with her that night. What kind of car did she own?"

"It was a pearly white Subaru," Brynn said.

Calero's high heels clicked as she moved toward the jury.

"How would you describe the relationship between the defendant and your brother?"

Brynn shrugged. "They were friends."

"Just friends?"

"They'd known each other since our days at SMU together. Deidra and Vance dated off and on through the years."

"Did that relationship change in the months leading up to the shooting?"

"Vance moved in with Deidra. I don't know whose idea it was, but I do know that they shared a bed. Vance was like Deidra's go-to boyfriend."

"Go-to boyfriend?" Calero asked for clarification.

"If no one better happened by, Vance would do," Brynn said.

"Did they relate as boyfriend and girlfriend on the night of the lake house party?"

"That's hard to say," Brynn said. "Deidra had grown terribly distraught. I do know that they argued that night."

"Argued?"

"Vance followed Deidra down to the dock. It was getting dark, and I didn't pay much attention to them, but I could hear them arguing."

"Do you remember what you overheard?"

"I heard Vance shout something to the effect that if she was that scared, she should dye her hair a different color, get a pair of glasses, and disguise herself."

"And then what happened?"

"Vance started up the hill toward the house."

"Is that when the gun was fired?"

Her eyes watering, Brynn said, "Yes."

"Would you say Mr. Montgomery was moving quickly, or did he walk slowly?"

"Not quickly." Brynn shook her head. "Vance was wearing a walking boot on one foot. He had broken his leg about five weeks earlier."

John Garrett stood to cross-examine Brynn Montgomery; he asked, "Did Vance and Deidra argue a lot?"

"Some," she said. "They would bicker back and forth about things."

"What kind of things?"

"Little things."

"Do you recall either of them physically harming the other?"

"No."

"Were either of them ever charged with domestic violence?"

"No."

"Do you recall times when they would argue loudly in public?"

"No."

"Thank you; no further questions."

"Who are these people?" Grace asked Monica Garrett when they recessed for lunch. "I don't know any of them, yet they are testifying to things I supposedly did and said."

"In your former life," Monica explained, "you knew them. That is, Deidra Wentworth knew them. All memory of them and the events they recall have been erased from your brain."

"And that will be our defense," John pointed out.

"It's frightening every time I remember that this Deidra Wentworth was me."

"Try to relax," Monica suggested. "Nothing is settled yet."

Back in the courtroom, Calero called Lee Holland to the witness stand. He was a tall, smartly dressed man.

"What do you do for a living?" the DA asked.

"I am a private investigator," Holland stated.

"How do you know the defendant?"

"Miss Wentworth and Vance Montgomery asked me to assist them after she had received several threatening messages."

"When was that?"

"It was in the spring of 2016."

"Were you able to uncover the source of the threats?"

"Eventually. I discovered that Sterling Wentworth, the defendant's deceased father, was deep in debt to several loan sharks."

"You stated that Miss Wentworth had received threats. Were any of these threats carried through? Was she ever in any real danger?"

"Objection! Opinion," Garrett called out.

"As Mr. Holland is an expert witness and hired by the defendant," Judge Sloane said, "I think it important for the jury to hear his opinion. Overruled."

"She might have been in grave danger. I advised her to never go anywhere alone. There was an incident while leaving work, she discovered that her tires had been slashed."

"Was there ever any money exchanged for these debts?" Calero asked.

"There was. She was instructed to deliver fifty thousand dollars to Globe Life Park. I accompanied her along with Vance Montgomery. Police presence was arranged. The money was taken from Miss Wentworth's person without her noticing. However, it was through that exchange that the police and I were able to establish the identity of these loan sharks. In fact, it broke open a significant ring."

When John Garrett stood to cross examine, he asked, "On what date were these loan sharks apprehended?"

"They were apprehended on June 5, 2016."

"The same day Vance Montgomery was shot and killed," Garrett said. "To your knowledge, had Miss Wentworth been advised of their apprehension before the time of the lake house party?"

"I sent her a message at 9:31 p.m. So no, she would not have received word."

"Are you saying that at the time of the shooting, Deidra Wentworth was still in the grips of fearing for her life?"

"She was."

"And you have testified that she had every reason to be afraid."

"That's right," Holland confirmed. "Miss Wentworth had paid these known extortionists for her father's gambling debts."

"Might such fear drive a person to violence?"

"Objection!"

By the time Grace returned to her cell, she was exhausted. She stretched out on her cot. "How can sitting in a chair all day be so tiring?" she asked Rhonda.

"Because everyone in the room is judging you," Rhonda pointed out. "Judgment is brutal."

"How about you? Has your sentence come down?"

Rhonda shook her head. "They're making me wait. Another way to torture people; they make you wait. I wish they'd tell me that I'm getting the damn needle."

"Maybe you won't be sentenced to death," Grace suggested.

Rhonda tossed her a disgusted look. "I've been convicted of murder."

"First degree or second degree?" Grace asked.

"There is no second degree in Texas. Only murder. On top of that, they got me for tampering with evidence, so they might as well give me the needle and be done with it."

That night, Grace lay limp on her cot, her mind running full speed. She had faced a room full of people she did not know, who were there to judge her. Poor Rhonda; after giving all for her son, she was convinced she will get the death sentence. Jewel, an innocent child, is accused of raping the only person to ever treat her kindly, while her own child was snatched from her. The bleakness of this awful place hit Grace like lightning, sending a spark down her spine. People were here for crimes they had committed, and yet every person Grace talked to left her with only sympathy for them. She wished she were back in the hospital, hooked up to tubes, but surrounded by people who cared. What had happened to her second chance in life?

Defendant

An uncomfortable familiarity enveloped Grace as she entered the courtroom the next day. The jury appeared tired. Santa Claus kept yawning. Taking her place, she was met with a flicker of hope. In the back row of the courtroom sat Jess Flynn, Dr. Milton, and Adelle Hall. The sight of friendly faces unleashed a load of inner tension like a balloon releasing its air. Grace could feel the support of her three friends as if warmth touched her from behind.

The prosecution called Susan Toll to the stand. The housekeeper's graying hair was tied back in a messy bun. Grace listened to her testimony.

"I have kept house for Sterling and Patricia Wentworth for twelve years," Susan stated. "Since Deidra was in high school."

"You've known the defendant for some time then," Calero said.

"I have. She had her father wrapped around her little

finger. She could get anything out of Sterling Wentworth, including her job at Alastair-Borne Publishing. And her mother … The girl's goal in life was to upset Patricia. They argued endlessly."

"Objection," John Garrett shouted. "This witness is expressing her opinion about things that have nothing to do with what happened on June 5, 2016."

"Sustained," Judge Sloane declared. "Please respond only to the questions you are asked."

"In the time you have been employed by the Wentworths, have you witnessed any tension between Deidra Wentworth and Vance Montgomery?"

Susan looked disgusted and said, "Almost every day."

"Explain what you observed."

"Deidra and Vance were both spoiled brats. She never had to work for anything, and he believed that the world revolved around him."

"Objection, again …"

"Keep your responses within the line of questioning," the judge emphasized.

"What was the question?" Susan asked.

Calero repeated, "Did you ever witness any tension between Deidra and Vance?"

"They fought constantly. They could not have a conversation without being interrupted by his damned cell phone. Oh, pardon my French. Deidra was so unappreciative of anything Vance tried to do for her."

"Can you give a specific example?"

"Once, Vance asked me to help him prepare a special dinner for her. Of course, she got home late and was angry that he had arranged the meal without first consulting her. They argued ceaselessly about money and her fears."

Calero said, "Your witness."

John Garrett began, "Ms. Toll, did you ever witness violence between Deidra and Vance?"

"No."

Before she could elaborate, John jumped to his next question: "Did you ever have to call the police or an ambulance because of either of them?"

"No, but the night Vance broke his leg, they had a party. I do not know what happened. How does a grown man fall down the stairs?"

"Your Honor?" Garrett addressed the judge.

"Strike that last statement from the record," the judge said.

Garrett spoke to the witness again: "Were you aware of Sterling Wentworth's gambling debts?"

"No. I am shocked."

"Did you observe Deidra in a fearful state?"

"A moody state," Susan replied. "She quit going to work. She quit going anywhere. I just assumed she was being difficult."

"No more questions." John returned to his seat.

Blaire Montgomery sat upright in the witness stand. Her shoulder-length red hair shone as radiantly as her huge, sparkling earrings. She was another person Grace did not know.

"How do you know Deidra Wentworth?" Calero asked.

"Deidra is a friend of my children, Brynn and Vance."

"Have you ever known her to be violent or to put someone in harm's way?"

"She kidnapped my daughter," Blaire snapped.

There was an audible gasp from the jury.

"Please explain," the district attorney invited.

"A week after Brynn and Deidra graduated from high school, Miss Wentworth whisked my daughter off to Europe. She did not tell me anything. She just disappeared. I found out from Patricia Wentworth. Lawrence and I were furious. That is why when Vance broke his leg that night, I couldn't help but wonder what really happened."

"Do you suspect that Deidra pushed him?"

"Objection! Leading the witness."

"Sustained."

A midday break was a welcome relief for Grace. As the courtroom emptied, she tried to catch the eyes of her friends at the back of the room. Dr. Milton had already stepped out, and Jess was adjusting her handbag. It was Adelle who looked up in her direction. Adelle's wide smile melted Grace's anxiety. Adelle paused and quickly patted her own heart. Instantly, Grace knew it was a gesture of love.

Returning for the afternoon session, Calero called India Morelli to the stand. Grace recognized her as the woman who had visited her with Monica. She had seemed kind and caring during their brief encounter.

Through the questioning, it was established that India had been a lifelong friend to Deidra. Their childhood friendship had stretched through college and beyond.

"I hated to see Deidra grow increasingly fearful. She wasn't herself anymore."

"Did you ever see her harm another person?" Calero asked.

"Never intentionally," India whispered.

"Speak up, please," the DA requested.

"Never intentionally."

"Tell us about the April 2016 party at the Wentworth home. Describe the mood of the party."

"The party was well planned by Vance, Brynn, and me. It was supposed to be a way to help Deidra relax and have some fun. Vance told Brynn and me that Deidra had agreed to the party idea."

"Was that the truth?"

"Apparently not. Deidra was terribly upset when she saw everybody at the house. We found out later that Deidra had informed Vance that she did not want a party."

"What happened next?"

"There was drinking and gaming. Then Vance invited everyone upstairs to see the newly redecorated bedroom."

"Continue."

"Deidra only wanted to sleep. She was exhausted from fear, so she demanded everyone leave the room and move back downstairs."

"Is that when Vance fell down the stairs?"

India nodded.

"Yes or no?"

"Yes."

"Did you see Deidra push him? Remember, you are under oath."

Reluctantly, India spoke. "She didn't mean to. I saw her give him a gentle shove from the top of the stairs, and he lost his balance."

"No more questions." Calero took her seat.

John Garrett stood. "Miss Morelli, was Vance Montgomery intoxicated at the time he fell from the top of the stairs?"

"Yes, he was. We had all been drinking."

"Was he staggering around?"

"Yes."

"Speaking in a slurred voice?"

"Yes."

"So Vance might have fallen, even if he had not been pushed?"

"Objection," Calero said. "Leading the witness."

"Sustained," said the judge.

~

The witness was a lanky, rather awkward man. He wore a button-down shirt with an undershirt showing at the neckline. His short hair was combed toward his forehead. His pleasant voice sounded rather soothing.

"Deidra and I were colleagues for seven years," Arthur Wexler began. "We both worked for Alistair-Borne Publishing House."

"Did Miss Wentworth discuss her personal life with you?"

"Not often."

"Did she talk about Vance Montgomery?"

"After her parents died, she told me that she let Vance move in with her."

"Was she excited about it?" Calero asked.

"Not really," Arthur answered. "She expressed it as more of an obligation."

"Drudgery?"

"Not drudgery, just not a deep commitment. I remember

the day Deidra told me that sometimes Vance was in the way, and that maybe she'd be better off without him."

"Were those her exact words?" the attorney asked.

"Maybe not her exact words. I mean, it has been over four years. But it was the thought she communicated to me. As she grew more and more fearful, I worried that Vance may have been abusive to her, but she assured me that was not the case."

Grace felt overwhelmed. Witness after witness testified to her moody, unappreciative, fearful personality. She had been seen pushing someone down the stairs and pulling the trigger of a gun. Who was she? Who had she been before awakening from the coma? Then she heard words that brought her back to the moment:

"The prosecution rests."

The moment Grace returned to the high-profile pod, Jewel scurried up to her.

"Grace, you come. Hurry, Grace."

"What is it?"

"It's the Rhonda lady."

When Grace reached her cell, she found Rhonda fighting hysterics. She swung her arm around her cellmate's shoulder and grabbed her hands.

"Calm down, Rhonda. Tell me what happened."

Grace rocked her back and forth. Gradually, Rhonda calmed down until they dropped side-by-side on Rhonda's hard cot.

"What happened?" Grace asked.

"Everything hit me all at once," Rhonda confessed. "I

was calm. I was calm when the judge handed down the sentence. I knew it was coming. So why did it hit me now?"

Grace felt her heart skip a beat. She whispered, "Are you getting the needle?"

Rhonda wiped her nose on her green and white striped shoulder. "No," she said. "I'm not getting the needle."

"That's a relief," Grace sighed.

"It should be. But I feel so defeated."

"What was the sentence?"

Rhonda stood and began to pace the cell. "For murder, I got forty years. For tampering with evidence, another twenty."

"Sixty years in prison?"

"I can serve them simultaneously, but Grace, I'm forty-seven years old. In forty years, I'll be eighty-seven. I really wish I got the needle," Rhonda shouted. "I really do."

"Surely not," Grace said.

"It's true," Rhonda continued. "Whenever a person dies, people have to blame someone. Not one of those people in that courtroom ever met James. They never scurried around, removing heavy objects and sharps so he wouldn't hurt himself or me. All those people know is that a young man died and was buried. And because of that, someone must pay. They have no idea how much I paid every day of James's life. Sometimes, this so-called justice is not fair."

Defendant

Grace did not spend much time in the day room. She would occasionally play cards with Jewel or work on a puzzle. When two of the inmates ran to her cell, calling for Grace to come, she knew something important was happening.

"They're talking about you on the news," they told her. "Hurry!"

A local newscaster touted an interview about the Deidra Wentworth case. Suddenly, a close-up shot revealed the faces of Blaire and Lawrence Montgomery.

"We are still heartbroken," Blaire was saying, acting as if she were fighting back tears.

"He was our only son," Lawrence added.

"To think of Deidra Wentworth going free makes me physically ill," Blaire continued.

"I'm sure it's been a long four years for you since the

murder. Will you be relieved when it's over?" the reporter asked.

"We need a sense of closure for sure," Lawrence said.

Blaire dabbed the corners of her eyes. "Our son is dead, and somebody must pay the price. Like the Bible says, 'An eye for an eye and a tooth for a tooth.'"

"Is it true that the defense is pushing an amnesia claim?" the reporter interjected.

Both Montgomerys nodded, and Lawrence said, "The fingerprints match those on the weapon. The DNA is a match. What more could they need to go on?"

"Can they legally grant that interview while the trial is on?" Grace asked.

"They just did," someone responded.

Grace entered the courthouse through the side door between Monica and John Garrett. On the front lawn, they could see a small cluster of picketers. People carried signs. "Runaway Rich Girl Go Straight to Jail" and "Justice for Vance" were among the messages.

"Don't look their direction," Monica advised her. "Keep walking and don't give them a thought."

"Won't this influence the jury?" Grace asked.

"The jury is sequestered. They won't know about it," Monica assured her client.

Grace's tensions were eased when she saw Jess and Adelle in the back of the courtroom again. When John Garrett called Dr. Dean Milton to the witness stand, she relaxed even more.

The doctor stated that he was a neurosurgeon practicing in Wichita, Kansas.

"What education is required to be a neurosurgeon?" Garrett asked.

"I took four years of medical school at the University of Kansas School of Medicine and six years neurosurgical residency at Grand Medical Center in Columbus, Ohio. I am certified by the American Board of Neurologic Surgery."

"How long have you practiced?"

"Thirty-four years of practice," the doctor stated.

Grace thought she caught a sparkle in Dr. Milton's eye shoot her direction.

"Describe for the court the defendant's condition when she arrived at St. Rafael Hospital on June 6, 2016."

Dr. Milton cleared his throat. "She was breathing through a tube. She presented with a significant indentation of the left temporal area of the skull and bleeding heavily. I recall she had a fractured humerus and deep lacerations to the left side of the face and upper leg."

"Was she responsive?"

"Absolutely not."

"Was surgery required?" John asked.

"Surgery was essential. Her brain was critically traumatized. Surgery allowed me to clean up the damaged area and repair the skull."

"So you removed part of the defendant's brain?" Garrett asked.

"Essentially," Dr. Milton confirmed. "We kept her in a coma to allow a certain amount of healing to take place."

Grace heard a stifled sniffle come from Adelle Hall.

"How long was the defendant in a coma?"

"Four weeks. We slowly brought her out of it."

"And when she came out of the coma? What was her condition at that point?"

Dr. Milton let out a deep sigh. "Confused. Unable to speak. Unable to move much."

"Did she know who she was?"

"You have to understand that the part of Grace's brain that was destroyed in the accident is the part that contained her episodic memory."

"Episodic memory?" Garrett asked.

"That's the part of the brain that stores personal experiences. She remembered nothing. Had no idea where she was, how she got there, or who she was."

"Is this normal for this type of condition?"

"It is a miracle that in this type of condition, Grace is not dead. Her chances of survival were minimal at most. She's a strong person, but she remembers nothing of her pre-accident life."

"How often have you encountered this kind of damage to the temporal lobe of the brain?"

"Never," confessed the doctor. "In thirty-four years of practice, I have never encountered damage to the temporal lobe this severe."

Garrett switched on a projector. "I think it is important for the jury to understand what Dr. Milton is describing here." A photo of Grace's mangled skull was projected onto a large screen. "Tell us about this image, Dr. Milton."

"This is Grace's condition upon arrival." The next slide showed her open skull during surgery. "Here, I'm clearing the destroyed tissue."

Groans and gulps arose in the courtroom.

"I object," Calero shouted. "This is prejudicial."

Garrett replied, "It's important for the jury to understand the depth of damage done to the defendant's brain."

"Wrap it up," the judge ordered.

Garrett continued, "In summary, Doctor, you are telling us that Grace's amnesia is extremely serious and very real."

"That's correct."

Judge Sloane called a brief recess before the prosecution cross-examined Dr. Milton. After the break, Calero positioned herself directly in front of the doctor, looking him in the eye.

"You testified that when the defendant came out of the coma, she was unable to speak, walk, or even move much. But she's doing it today."

"Gradually her body repaired. It was a slow and determined recovery, requiring a lot of time and hard work."

"She can't remember who she is, you say?"

"Correct."

"Yet she can still read, drive, count money, and play piano. Her injuries didn't affect those abilities?"

"As I have said, the part of Grace's brain that was destroyed contained her episodic declarative memory, which means her personal experiences. Those no longer exist. Her procedural memory encompasses motion skills, such as how to drive a car and play the piano."

"Does she remember the meaning of words, for example?"

"The meaning of words, the recall of facts, and basic common knowledge is part of her semantic memory, which is mostly still undamaged."

"This sounds terribly complicated," Calero said. "Could you say it in simpler terms?"

Dr. Milton cleared his throat again. "Simply stated, there are two types of memory: declarative and procedural. Procedural includes motor skills and the use of objects. Declarative memory is divided into episodic memory and semantic memory. Semantic memory has to do with recall of facts and common knowledge. Episodic memory has to do with specific events and personal history. It is the episodic memory that was completely destroyed in Grace's accident and subsequent surgery."

"Is there actually a name for this condition?"

"It is called complete declarative amnesia. Although it's more accurately termed complete declarative episodic amnesia."

"The body is an amazing machine," Calero remarked. "If the motor skills repaired themselves over time, wouldn't it be reasonable that memory skills could do that as well? Given enough time."

The doctor smiled and shook his head. "Grace's personal memory has been erased. Forever."

Dr. Ted Yates took his place on the witness stand. His long white hair was tied back in a ponytail. He wore nicely creased khaki pants with his traditional denim shirt. John Garrett established the psychiatrist's credibility by having him state that he had graduated from Perelman School of Medicine at the University of Pennsylvania and had done four years postgraduate residency training at the Hospital of the University of Pennsylvania.

"How do you know the defendant?"

"I met Grace Shepard while she was a patient at St. Rafael and continued working with her at Crestway Rehab Center and beyond."

"How long was Grace your client?"

"Two years on a regular basis," Dr. Ted said.

"What can you tell us about her mental state?"

"Ms. Shepard was kind but confused. She had no recollection of her identity. We spent considerable time grieving the life she had no memory of. She was unaware of any family, had no friends except those she met at the hospitals, no childhood, no education."

"Did she ever come across as violent?" Garrett asked.

"Never," Yates said. "In fact, quite the opposite. She was a fighter in her recovery but never physically. She fought for everything she has accomplished in the past four years. Building a new identity was a huge challenge. I used to tell her to take one step at a time."

"Do you recall her ever remembering something from her past? A name? A place?"

Dr. Ted thought for a moment. "No. Never."

"Did you ever try hypnosis?"

"We did. Ms. Shepard was willing to try it."

"And? Was memory uncovered?"

Dr. Ted shook his head. "Nothing. Hypnosis can be a useful tool for recall. In Ms. Shepard's case, there was nothing left to reveal."

"No further questions," Garrett said.

The district attorney approached Dr. Ted and asked, "Isn't amnesia easy to fake?"

"It can be easy to fake loss of memory of a single event. Perhaps a memory of violence or a crime. Extensive memory, however, is hard to fake, especially for a four-year period."

"Isn't it true," Calero asked, "that many people suppress a traumatic experience, forgetting it ever happened?"

"There is a huge difference between suppressing a memory and losing the memory altogether. A suppressed memory remains in the subconscious brain. It often surfaces through therapy or hypnosis. In Ms. Shepard's case, there is no memory left to come to the surface."

"No further questions."

That night, Monica and John carefully led Grace out the side door of the courthouse. She did not look, but she could tell by the voices that the number of demonstrators had grown.

"They don't know what happened. And they certainly do not know you," John told her. "They are demonstrating against a half-truth."

Grace felt a comfort on her cot that night. There were no demonstrators, there was no jury, and Rhonda was sleeping a few feet away.

Defendant

The courtroom had become hauntingly familiar while the protests outside continued to increase. Grace felt unsettled, anxious for the whole experience to be over. When John Garrett called Jessica Flynn to the witness stand, Grace's adrenaline began to flow.

Jess explained to the court that she was an occupational therapist from Crestway Rehabilitation Center in Wichita, Kansas.

"What does an occupational therapist do?" Garrett asked.

"We work with clients to develop their physical and mental skills required for daily living."

"When Grace first arrived at Crestway after being released from the hospital, how would you assess her memory skills?"

"Quite limited," Jess said. "She knew what to do with a bar of soap and a toothbrush, but the whole world appeared new to her. Of course, having been in the hospital for that length of time would make the world more vivid, I suppose."

"Could she recognize places of business? Shops? Offices?"

"She recognized McDonald's but had no memory of actually eating there. She remembered that a bank had to do with money but could not recall doing business in one. I helped her relearn physical skills and built up her strength. She practiced writing with a pencil, cooking, doing laundry, and using a computer. Her keyboard skills were relatively good."

"After her stay at Crestway, did you and Grace keep in touch?"

"Grace had nowhere to go upon leaving Crestway. The social worker was trying to have her placed in an assisted living facility. Grace and I hit it off so well that I invited her to come stay with me."

"How long did that living arrangement last?"

"Grace roomed with me for three years. After that, she was able to afford her own apartment in our complex."

"Did she help out with chores?" Garrett asked.

"Oh, yes," exclaimed Jess. "She cooked and cleaned. Grace made it clear that she wanted to pull her weight."

"She didn't expect to be waited on?"

"Absolutely not."

"Did Grace contribute to the household income?"

"Eventually. At first, a job was beyond her reach. She could prove no education, had no legal identification, and did not even have a Social Security number. She eagerly studied to earn her GED and went through all the steps to get a Social Security number, legal ID, and a driver's license. At that point, she got a job at Allegro Music Store in Wichita."

"How long was she employed at Allegro?"

"Until her arrest. She loved it there. Not only did she work the sales floor, but she gave music lessons as well. The owner of Allegro encouraged her to pursue a career in music. Grace was offered a full music scholarship to Whitbury College, where she was working toward a degree."

"You have known her for over three years," Garrett said. "Have you ever seen her express rage?"

"Never."

"Have you ever seen her violently upset?"

"Never."

"Thank you. No more questions." Garrett took his seat beside Grace.

Calero approached the witness. She gave Jess a puzzled look and asked, "What did the defendant do to find her identity?"

Jess looked perplexed. "What do you mean?"

"I mean, did she make inquiries about herself? Did she search on-line? Did she inquire about missing persons throughout the country?"

"I don't think so."

"Did she have her fingerprints taken and sent to law enforcement for identification purposes?"

"She was very curious about her past life," Jess said.

"Did she do any of those things?"

"No. But she did take a DNA test through Heritage.com to gain information about her ancestry."

"And it was that test that identified her as Deidra Wentworth, the killer of Vance Montgomery. No wonder she avoided other efforts." Garrett began to rise, but Calero said, "Withdrawn. Nothing further, Your Honor."

~

Returning from a midday recess, Monica Garrett leaned over to Grace. "I stepped outside for lunch," she told her client. "There are more demonstrators."

Grace rolled her eyes in disgust.

"No, it's a good thing," Monica pointed out. "This group is supporting you."

"Really?" Grace was astonished.

"It's a small group, but their signs read, 'Mercy for Grace' and 'Rich Girl is Dead.' I even saw one painted purple that said, 'We Love Amazing Grace.'"

"How do they even know what is happening in the courtroom?" Grace asked.

"Summaries are offered to the local news, and people make up the rest. I just want you to know that not everyone is against you."

"Thank you," Grace said, sighing.

"One more thing," Monica said. "Do you know who the man in the back row is?"

Grace turned to look. A quick gasp escaped her when she saw Jeremy Barton sitting in between Jess and Adelle.

"Somebody you know?" Monica asked.

"Oh yes. Definitely somebody I know." Grace smiled and rose as Judge Sloane entered the room. Did Jeremy come to support her or to see her convicted? She was afraid to assume his reasons. The momentary glimpse of Jeremy reminded Grace just how much she cared about him.

By the time her mind returned to the trial, John Garrett

was questioning David Edelman. "Have you assisted others in changing their identity?" he asked.

"I specialize in family law, which includes divorce, prenuptial agreements, adoptions, and identity changes."

"Are there a lot of people seeking to change their identity?"

Edelman chuckled. "Not many. Most of them are people who have come out of abusive, threatening relationships. Fearing their own safety, I help them establish a new identity so they cannot be found by their abuser."

"And in Grace Shepard's case?"

"Ms. Shepard's case was unique. She came to me with no identity at all. We had nothing to start with."

"Did you ever question whether her story was true?"

"Never," Edelman said. "She came with documentation from Dr. Dean Milton, Dr. Ted Yates, and Jessica Flynn, who was a friend and occupational therapist. I had never met anybody so void of self-identification. It proved quite a rewarding venture in my law career."

Calero's cross-examination was brief. "Did you sense the moral responsibility of taking on the Grace Shepard case?"

"Ma'am?" Edelman asked, confused.

"If a client asked to change her identity for the purpose of hiding from the law, wouldn't it be your responsibility to refuse services? Did you worry about becoming an accessory to a crime?"

"There was no evidence of the client hiding from anything or anyone."

"Your integrity was based on the word of one neurosurgeon and one psychiatrist?" Calero asked.

"Dr. Milton's word was accompanied by volumes of

medical documents and professional publications, as was Dr. Yates's. It was not the word of one surgeon and one psychiatrist; it was the word of the neurological and psychological communities. Without my help, Ms. Shepard could not drive, work, secure an education, or even vote. It was my moral obligation to give her a life to live."

With no more witnesses to be called to the stand, DA Calero approached the jury with her closing argument. Grace's nervousness increased, realizing that her fate rested in the hands of those twelve people. She observed their faces as the district attorney spoke.

"Ladies and gentlemen of the jury, it has been established that Deidra Wentworth received everything she wanted: her education, her job, her status, and her home. When it did not go her way, she took things into her own hands. Yes, Deidra Wentworth had been threatened, but didn't she also threaten Vance Montgomery?

"A party was planned to help her relax and have fun. In preparation, she loaded her gun, put it into her Gucci beach bag, and went to the party. With alcohol in her system, Deidra Wentworth left the gathering and led Vance Montgomery to the dock. She waited until it was dark and then took out her Springfield XDM handgun with all its safety features and shot him in cold blood. She intentionally killed Mr. Montgomery. His life snuffed out.

"Too cowardly to face the consequences, Deidra Wentworth abandoned her car, as though she had been abducted, and traveled north. As it happened, that escape ended in a fatal accident. Only Ms. Wentworth survived the crash. Landing in the hospital in a city two states away, it was the perfect opportunity to fake amnesia and construct a new identity. I am not saying she did not have some memory loss, but the odds of complete declarative amnesia are extremely minute. Almost impossible odds.

"Forensic science reveals the truth. DNA cannot be changed. Fingerprints cannot be changed. All evidence points to her as the killer. Vance Montgomery is dead. His family has been grieving for four years. Ladies and gentlemen, justice must be served. Yes, Ms. Wentworth lost some memory, but Mr. Montgomery lost his life. Just because an event is erased from memory does not mean it never happened. Doctors have testified that she never lost her ability to read, drive, play the piano, and I assure you; she remembers how to kill."

The courtroom was eerily still as Calero clicked back to her seat. Her job complete, she sat tall and confident, with a look of satisfaction on her face.

John Garrett stood and rolled up his shirt sleeves, as if preparing for work. He took a moment to look at each member of the jury. "Sitting before you is a woman who has experienced a trauma most people never know, no less understand. Yes, a man was killed. He was shot with a gun, and Deidra Wentworth pulled the trigger. She had been threatened repeatedly. She was scared. Still grieving the loss of both parents, and fearing for her own life, Deidra Wentworth lived in raw fear. She sought the help of a private investigator. She was not out to get the victim. She did not carry the gun for the purpose of murder; she carried it for self-defense against an unknown loan shark. The idea that she somehow planned the shooting is pure speculation, with no basis in fact and no evidence to prove it.

"The same fear that provoked her to shoot, sent her running from the scene. It led her, however, not to safety but to a fatal accident. A traumatic brain injury left her in a coma and extinguished all memory of her earlier life.

"From that moment, Grace Shepard worked fiercely for everything she needed. She struggled to speak and to walk. She sought an education from scratch. She took a minimal job and worked her way up. She did it with no rich parents, no mansion, no well-established name.

"I am convinced that on June 6, 2016, that fatal accident killed not just two people but three. In the early morning of that day, Deidra Wentworth died. Deidra Wentworth no longer exists. Her memory is gone. Relationships are gone. Her history is wiped out. Her life was snuffed out by a brutal brain injury.

"The person who sits before you is not Deidra Wentworth, but Grace Shepard. Grace Shepard is a musician, a student, a clerk in a store, living in a modest apartment in Wichita, Kansas. Until her arrest, she had no knowledge of Vance Montgomery.

"The life of Vance Montgomery was taken. The life of Deidra Wentworth was also taken. Grace Shepard is in no way guilty of murder. Do we ruin another life in the guise of justice? Do we truly seek justice, or do we simply want to get even?

"An eye for an eye? A tooth for a tooth? A life for a life – the sacrifice has already been made. Deidra Wentworth may have been guilty of manslaughter, but not murder. And Grace Shepard is as innocent as anyone in this room."

John Garrett wiped sweat from his brow. He took a

deep breath as he established eye contact with the jury once again.

"We are so willing to justify punishment, but this case calls us to justify mercy. I am hard-pressed to think of a situation where it would be more prudent to seek mercy. Deidra's life is over. Grace's life has only just begun. By the mercy in your hearts, allow her a chance to live, to blossom, to give something back to this world."

Grace wiped tears from her eyes. Although she could not see it, Jess and Jeremy were doing the same thing.

After Garrett sat down, Judge Sloane charged the jury and then dismissed them for the night. Deliberations would begin in the morning.

Defendant

The jury commenced deliberation at seven o'clock the next morning. John and Monica Garrett apprised Grace that there was no telling how long the process would take.

"Try to relax. We'll call when the time comes."

Relaxation evaded Grace. Her fate rested in the hands of twelve strangers. She had never felt so lonely. How long had it been since she had a conversation with somebody about something other than crime and court? How long had it been since she touched another person in a way other than sympathy? It seemed forever. She lay on her cot, reviewing the four years since she awoke from the coma. Such wonderful care she had received from people she knew nothing about: Dr. Milton, Adelle, Dr. Ted, Jess, Jeremy, Janet Price, and Dr. Oglesbee. Complete strangers had given her a new life. Would another group of strangers take it away?

Grace refused to step into the day room for fear the news would broadcast a story about her case. Jewel was gone with her court-appointed attorney, who was trying to arrange a plea bargain. She thought about the people who passed in and out of the high-profile pod. The latest arrival, shaken with drug withdrawal, had been whisked off to correctional health services. Grace did not even know her name.

The morning slid into afternoon. Grace found herself either pacing the hall or trying to sleep. Neither activity resolved her anxiety. Shortly after three o'clock, an officer aroused her from near-sleep.

"Time to go," she said. "The jury has reached a verdict."

Surprised and startled from her nap, Grace asked. "Can I brush my teeth first?"

"They need you now."

Grace was ushered to the courthouse, where she met Monica Garrett. A quick change into freshly pressed slacks and a loose-fitting blouse, a brush through her hair, and she was ready to join John in the courtroom.

The jury filed in.

"Have you reached a verdict?" Judge Sloane asked.

"We have," spoke the foreman, a stout little man positioned beside the young Hispanic juror.

"Will the defendant please rise?"

Grace's hands shook as she rose to her trembling feet, held aloft by a Garrett on either side.

"In the case of the *State of Texas versus Deidra Wentworth*," the foreman read. "For the charge of murder, we the jury find Deidra Wentworth not guilty."

A groan came from the Montgomerys in the courtroom; gasps could be heard from the last row.

"For the charge of manslaughter," the foreman continued. "We find Deidra Wentworth guilty."

A mumble of responses swelled through the courtroom.

"The court shall come to order," the judge commanded.

To Grace's surprise, the foreman continued, "In addition, for the charge of murder, we find Grace Shepard not guilty. For the charge of manslaughter, we find Grace Shepard not guilty."

Confusion swept over Grace. "What does this mean?" she asked John.

"This is unprecedented," he exclaimed.

Monica said, "The jury obviously identified two separate defendants, despite the judge's opening words. Now we wait for sentencing."

~

Grace sat in the visitor's room, thrilled for the moment she had awaited since her arrest. Jeremy Barton sat on the other side of the glass, a receiver at his ear. He had the same gentle eyes and relaxed brown hair. Clad in a school polo, he spoke Grace's name.

"Grace, I am so sorry."

"I'm sorry too. I should have told you about the accident and amnesia."

"I should have trusted you," he apologized. "It was so shocking."

"I'm glad you came," Grace confessed.

"When Jess explained the ordeal, I needed time to process it. The thing is ..." His voice drifted off.

"Yes?"

"The thing is, after you were taken away, I realized that I love you."

Grace sat speechless.

"Did you hear me?" he asked.

Grace nodded.

"I have missed you so much, Grace. Whether you go to prison for one month or ten years, I will be here for you. I mean it."

Grace's eyes glazed over. "How I wish I could kiss you right now." Her voice was thick with emotion.

Slowly, Jeremy placed his hand on the glass that separated them. Grace mirrored the gesture. She imagined that she could feel the warmth of his touch.

"I love you too, Jeremy," Grace said, smiling even as tears crept down her cheeks.

Awaiting sentencing was more agonizing than awaiting the verdict. Puzzled beyond understanding, Grace was afraid to imagine what the split verdict meant for her. A new cellmate arrived but disappeared as quickly as she came. Grace was fueled solely by her visits from Jeremy and Jess.

"Let's think about this," Jess suggested from the other side of the glass. "The jury admitted that Grace and Deidra are two different people."

"But we occupied the same body," Grace reminded her friend. "How can one be imprisoned for manslaughter while the other goes free?"

"You're confusing me, Grace."

"The entire case is confusing, and I don't know what to think. The Garretts tell me that the sentencing could come down anytime from tomorrow to two months from now.

I agree with the person who said the waiting is a means of torture."

∽

On the day of sentencing, rain pummeled Dallas. Grace tried to run into the courthouse under the edge of Monica Garrett's umbrella. Soaked by the time she stepped inside, she feared that the weather might be an omen to her future. Seated in front of Judge Sloane once again, Grace heard thunder roll over the building like a slow-moving wrecking ball.

Judge Murray Sloane spoke with precision. "For the conviction of manslaughter, which is a second-degree felony, I sentence Deidra Wentworth to a fine of ten thousand dollars." He paused briefly before continuing. "In addition, I recommend for Deidra Wentworth a speedy Declaration of Presumed Death.

"As restitution, Deidra Wentworth will provide Grace Shepard a monetary sum that will cover attorney costs and medical expenses. After that, Grace Shepard will have no claim to the Wentworth estate."

The courtroom remained still as death itself. Gradually, people realized that Deidra Wentworth would be declared dead, while Grace Shepard had been granted a second chance to live.

The headline in the *Dallas Daily Reporter* read "Runaway Rich Girl to be Declared Dead."

∽

Grace lay back in the airplane seat between Jess and Jeremy. She was headed to the only home she could remember.

Finally relaxed, she slept peacefully through the forty-five-minute flight.

One month later, a small group of people gathered in the Quinley Park Cemetery. Among them stood India Morelli, Brynn Montgomery, Arthur Wexler, Susan Toll, and others who had known Deidra. At their feet rested a granite slab that read: *Deidra Wentworth, 1987–2016.*

"She was a good friend," India sighed.

"I really miss her," Brynn confessed.

Arthur Wexler placed a cluster of daisies next to the headstone. He read a short poem and then invited the assembly to share memories.

On that same day in Wichita, Kansas, dressed in his best suit, Jeremy Barton walked Grace Shepard up the steps of the Whitbury College Auditorium. Grace wore a new emerald green tea dress.

"Isn't it early for their seasonal concert?" Grace asked.

"This season is special," he explained.

Inside, Grace noticed that there was no one in the lobby.

"Are you sure it's tonight?" she asked.

"Positive," he said, grinning and clasping her hand.

Walking through the double doors, Grace met a packed audience. They stood as she and Jeremy made their entrance. The Whitbury Symphonic Orchestra filled the stage; they began playing a familiar piece. Jeremy ushered her down the aisle, and Dr. Wesley Oglesbee brought the music to a sudden halt. He stepped to the microphone.

"Ladies and gentlemen, we've assembled here tonight, not for a seasonal concert, but for the purpose of welcoming Grace Shepard back to Wichita and to Whitbury. Grace, we have prayed for you, and tonight we play for you. But for some reason, we do not sound quite complete. Would you do the honor of joining us?"

Dr. Oglesbee held out a shiny silver flute and extended it toward Grace. "It's yours," he explained. "And it's felt very neglected."

Jeremy kissed Grace on the cheek as she made her way up to the stage.

"I'm out of practice," she said shyly.

She took the only empty seat in the orchestra, lifted the instrument to her lips, then lost herself in "Concerto for Flute and Orchestra No. 1 in G Major," every note stored in her brain. The music embraced her, carrying her soul to new heights. She knew she was home.

After a lavish reception, Grace and Jeremy walked the campus. Bathed in moonlight, they sat on a bench under the quaking leaves of a cottonwood tree. Jeremy took her hands in his.

"Grace Shepard," he said. "You are the best thing to ever happen to me. You are talented and bright, determined and kind. I love you."

He moved toward her until their lips touched in a deep, passionate kiss.

"I love you too," she whispered between kisses.

"I love your soft, brown hair and the sparkle in your grey eyes," he breathed.

"Do you love my scars? I try to hide them, but ..."

Jeremy placed a finger to her lips, his face beaming with adoration. "I especially love your scars. Don't hide them. It was your scars that brought us together."

That night, Grace snuggled into her bed at Lakewood Villa Apartments. Warm and comfortable, she knew that

Jess was upstairs and Mrs. Bellamy down the hall. Music lingered in her mind, as did the memory of Jeremy's touch. She drifted toward sleep, knowing she was home, she was loved, and she was safe.

Acknowledgments

My thanks go to the following people:

To Jonathan Hogg, who enthusiastically allowed me to bounce ideas off him. To Kathy Whitley, my volunteer proofreader. To family members Ryan McLain, Chris McLain, Laura, and Timothy Snell, whose ideas and opinions I respect. Most of all, to my husband, Allen, who witnessed the evolution of a story, assisted with medical information, and put up with my questions and imagination.

About the Author

Barbara McLain is a retired United Methodist minister. Besides pastoring several churches throughout Kansas, she has directed and taught preschool as well as public speaking for a community college. Barbara lives in Ransom, Kansas, with her husband. They enjoy visiting their grown children and spoiling their grandchildren.

CPSIA information can be obtained
at www.ICGtesting.com
Printed in the USA
BVHW081939130421
604813BV00005B/406